Sun Journey

Sun Journey

A Story of Zuni Pueblo

by

Ann Nolan Clark

Illustrated by

Percy Tsisete Sandy

Ancient City Press
Santa Fe, New Mexico

© Copyright 1988 by Ancient City Press. For information
address Ancient City Press, P.O. Box 5401, Santa Fe, New Mexico 87502.

Zuni bird and pottery designs used with permission from
Decorative Art of the Southwestern Indians by Dorothy Smith Sides,
Dover Publications, New York.

International Standard Book Number:
ISBN 0-941270-49-1 Hardbound
ISBN 0-941270-48-3 Paperback
Library of Congress Catalogue Number:
88-070955

Second Ancient City Press Printing

Designed by Mary Powell
Cover design by Ellen Fox

Contents

Zuni Calendar   1
Winter Solstice   3
Making Prayer Sticks   9
Planting Prayer Sticks   13
New-Fire   15
Little Stone Wild Cat   19
Big Fire Eater   21
Baby Eagles   27
Planting Time   33
Stick Race   35
Uncle Goes to the Salt Lakes   41
Summer Solstice   45
New Learning   49
Harvest   53
Gathering the Wild Plants   59
Other Things To Do   63
Knowledge   67
Zuni Games   71
Waiting for Shalako   73
Shalako   75
Back to the Middle-Place   81
The Artist Speaks for Himself   85

Zuni Calendar

"Grandfather! Grandfather! Wait for me. Grandfather. Please."

Black night hung low in Zuni. There were no stars. Snow was falling. It was piling thick and white on the sand and the pinon shrubs and the lonesome fields.

Coyotes barked near the foot of Sacred Mountain. Their barking broke the night into falling pieces. Their barking shattered the stillness and the blackness.

Two figures walked in the trail. One was tall. The other one was short. Both were wrapped in black blankets. Only their eyes peeped out. Only their moccasined feet seemed to move. They walked quickly. They made no sound. They were part of the night.

Tall One was leading. He was Grandfather Hotima, Indian Sun Priest of Zuni. Little One was Ze-do, Indian boy of Zuni.

Ze-do was sleepy and cold and his feet stumbled in the tracks of his Grandfather. He was not happy. He was not interested. He was uncomfortable and cross.

Grandfather was talking. His low voice sounded like drum music to the dancing snowflakes. His low voice sounded warm to the cold little boy. Grandfather's talking was like a strong hand held out to help him over the sharp rocks of the night-black trail.

Grandfather was talking. "You are now as my son. For three years you have gone to Government School. But this year has been given me to teach you of the ways of your own people. You are of an age to learn."

Ze-do thought longingly of the big Government School. He thought of the warm beds there, where he could now be sleeping. His feet were so cold. They felt like big, clumsy sticks. Perhaps his toes had broken off. He could not see them.

He looked up at his Grandfather, "I am ten years old. Perhaps, I should be in Government School."

Grandfather corrected him. "A Zuni does not count his age by each year, Grandson, but by each four. You are in your third four."

Ze-do listened, but he did not think what Grandfather was saying was very important. He kept saying to himself, as he stumbled along, "That is not the way to say it. I know how old I am. I am ten years old. Ten years old is the way to say it." But he did not speak aloud. Although he had been to White man's school a long time, he still remembered that Indian children never argue with Indian old men.

Behind them the terraced houses of

1

Zuni looked like stairstep shadows against the snow-swirling sky. Now they had reached the edge of Zuni village. Before them was a twisted petrified tree stump. This was the calendar of Zuni.

Zuni people do not have a picture calendar with the days of the week and the months of the year and numbers written on it for all to see. Zuni people have one man who keeps the calendar for them. This man was Grandfather, their Sun Priest, their Pek-kwi-neh, the holder of their road of light. He tells the people when winter begins, and summer.

Every morning Grandfather, the Sun Priest, goes to the petrified tree stump near the edge of the Zuni village. Near it he stands and watches the sun as it comes from behind the foothills between the mountains and the valley. Sun Carrier does not rise in the same place each morning and Grandfather knows this. He knows where Sun Carrier will rise when it is time for snow or for planting or for harvest. Grandfather is a wise old man. He must be wise, for it is his duty to count the days for his people.

All this Grandfather told the little Ze-do. All this and much more he told him as they walked along in the cold morning.

He told him that Zuni call their year Teh-pi-qui-yih; that the six months of winter make one season and the six months of summer make the other season. That the months have such names as growing-white-moon-time, boughs-broken-by-snow-time, snow-lies-not-in-the-trails-time and time-of-little-sand-storms and time-of-big-sand-storms.

Ze-do listened to all that his Grandfather told him. But he was thinking how cold he was, and how, if he were back at school, he would be in his warm bed. He looked up at his talking Grandafther and said, in a little voice that he tried very hard to make big, "At the Government School they think that when it is night, little boys should be in bed."

Grandafather put his hand on the boy's shoulder. His hand felt kind. It felt friendly. Grandafther was looking down at him. Ze-do could feel him looking down. Grandfather spoke as if he understood what a boy who had been to school was thinking. Grandfather said, "At school things are different. There White man teaches you his way. He wraps his feelings up in words and puts them with marks on paper for you to see. Here we keep our feelings in our hearts. To know them you must live them."

Grandfather said, "If you should ever be Sun Priest of Zuni how would you know to count the days for your people unless you had learned by doing it?"

Ze-do said, "I could look on a picture calendar, couldn't I, Grandfather?" And the old man answered, "No. The people have always done it this way."

Winter Solstice

Snow had stoppped falling, and grey morning had blotted out night blackness. The air smelled of pinon where the heavy snows had bruised the little trees. Nothing stirred. The coyotes had finished barking. There was deep stillness and hush and waiting. On a little hill a jack rabbit sat.

Grandfather and Ze-do reached the tree stump sun marker at the edge of Zuni village. Grandfather pointed. Slowly to the east he pointed. Softly he whispered, "Ah-h." Softly he breathed it, "Ah-h." Grandfather sounded happy. "Look," he said, "Look. The sun is coming."

Ze-do looked where Grandfather was pointing. He saw night clouds parting to let the colors of day come though. He saw a great red-yellow ball of fire. It was the sun. The sun came. With his blanket of many colors, with his warmth and with his light, he came over the foothills between the mountain and the valley.

Grandfather kept his hand raised, pointing. Higher and higher rose the red ball of fire. Then Grandfather turned and pointed to the southwestern corner of Sacred Mountain. Sun Father's fingers were touching there. They were making of Sacred Mountain a flaming stone.

"When Sun Carrier comes between those points of rocks," Grandfather explained, "when his fingers of light touch the end of Sacred Mountain then I know it is time for Winter Solstice. It is the time of the Zuni New Year. Thus it has been from the beginning. I brought you home from school at this time, Grandchild, so that you might be with me when Sun Father showed, by the place of his coming, that a new year must begin at Zuni. Now you have seen it. Now you know it."

Grandfather and Ze-do hurried back to Zuni.

The going home did not seem so long. It did not seem so cold. Even the icy breath of the terrible god of the North Wind was warmer, now that the sun was blessing the world with its light.

At the outskirts of the pueblo, Grandfather met the Crier. The Crier was an old man, but not, perhaps, as old as Grandfather. He was tall, but not as tall as Grandfather. His work was to stand on the top house of the biggest plaza and tell the news to the people. He must tell it in a loud voice so that all could hear him. A little after sunrise and a little after sunset were the times of the day that the Crier told his news.

Now, when Grandfather met the Crier he said to him, "The shortest day of the year is upon us." He said it in Zuni, like this, "Ya-tokian i-ti-wan-nan kwin-te-chi-kah." "Sun Father reaches the Middle-Place."

The Crier was glad to hear this. He went quickly to the top house on the biggest plaza. He stood on the roof of the house with his black blanket wrapped closely about him. He looked very tall and black standing there against the paleness of the morning sky. His voice cut a trail through the stillness of morning. He cried the news for all to hear. "Ya-tokian i-ti-wan-nan kwin-te-chi-kah."

Zuni woke up. Dogs barked. House doors were opened. Little blue curls of cedar smoke made breath puffs from the mouths of fat chimneys.

Grandfather took Ze-do into the house. It was a big room with snow white walls. The floor was of hard dirt, soft brown in color. Hanging down from the vigas across the ceiling were bunches of dried herbs and bunches of feathers and other things. Hanging on a pole against the wall were bright blankets that the Navajo had woven, and shawls and buckskins and a feathered headdress. On another pole was hung a bridle and a coil of rope, a saddle blanket and a saddle bag.

The fire in the fireplace looked good to Ze-do. He was glad to sit before its friendly warmth. Grandfather hung the little boy's blanket on the pole-for-the-soft-things. He put the little boy's moccasins on the hearth to dry. Then the old man rubbed snow on Ze-do's toes and on his fingers. The cold snow seemed to warm the cold toes and fingers. Little feelings like small thorn pricks came into them, but Grandfather rubbed and rubbed and soon the thorn prick feelings went away and the cold went away. Ze-do's toes and fingers were all

right again. They were warm again. They felt just as they always had felt before they were so cold.

Quatsia came from her house around the corner. She brought breakfast which she had cooked for them. She spread it on the floor nearby for them to eat. There was a basket of Zuni bread and an earthen pot of goat meat stew and chili and beans. Into the goat meat stew Grandfather crumbled dried thistle flowers. The thistle flowers were a special treat. Grandfather smiled at Ze-do. He said, "A special treat for a special day when the small Grandson saw Sun Father bringing the new year to the people."

Quatsia came back. She brought strong black coffee for them to drink. She brought sweets of uncooked deer fat wrapped in blankets of wild currant leaves.

It was good to be here. Ze-do felt dry and warm, full of good food and good thoughts. He was happy because Grandfather was happy. It was good to know that he had helped the Sun Priest read the Sun Father's message.

While they ate together, before the cheerful fire, Grandfather told the story of the Zuni people.

Grandfather said, "We are A'shi wi, the people. White men have many names for us. They call us Indians. Where they got that name I do not know. Perhaps those marks that they put in books may tell you that. They call our towns Pueblos. That word comes from the Spanish. It means houses built at one place, making a small town. They call us Pueblo Indians, Zuni, Red men, and many names. But as for us, we do not need names. We know who we are. We are the people."

"Long time ago, in the days-of-the old,

the A'shi wi wandered through many worlds all of them under this one. At last Sun Father sent his twin sons to lead the people up from their underworlds. The twin sons of Sun Father led the people up and up and up through the crust of this world where we are now living."

It was a long story. Grandfather's voice went on and on. The fire crackled and glowed. Little blue flames danced and played and hid away again in the coals. Blue cedar smoke filled the room with sweet smell and sleepy smoke mist.

Ze-do made little trips into the land of sleeping and came quickly back to his Grandfather's talking, so that he did not miss much of the story of Zuni.

It was the beginning of winter. Sun Father had said so. In his journey around the year he had stopped long enough to paint his light on Sacred Mountain. He had reached the Middle-Place. He had told this secret to the one man who must know it. He had told this secret to Grandfather who kept the days for the people.

Making Prayer Sticks

Snow water dripped down from the house tops. The mud walls of the houses turned dark brown with the wetness of the drip-drip-drip, trickling down the sides. The walls smelled good like warm thirsty earth, drinking.

Sacred Mountain looked shining and clean, all bare rock spotted with snow patches.

Zuni people walked fast, in and out doors, and up and down ladders. There was much work to be done, getting the new year started in Zuni. Water and fire wood were brought into the houses—enough to last for many days, because nothing is brought in or taken out of a house during Winter Solstice ceremony. Great quantities of food were bought at the Trading Post. For there can be no buying or selling during the Ceremony.

Meat stews were cooked and corn was ground into meal. Ceremonial bread was made and stored away in baskets and pottery storage jars.

Then came the time to make the sacred prayer sticks. Prayer sticks are made of the feathers of swift-flying birds. They are tied to painted willow wands with strings of colored yarns. Prayer sticks are wing prayers flying up through the Blue-Blue to the All-Fathers, who are the holders of the trails-of-living.

Grandfather went to his mother's house to make his prayer sticks. His mother had been dead for many years. But Grandfather went to her house for that was the right way of doing. He took Ze-do with him.

Many people were there at Grandfather's mother's house. She had been a woman of many sons and daughters. Ze-do was glad to see the people. He liked to be where there were many others. He had become used to that at Government School. Ze-do missed school. When he was cold, he missed it. When he was tired from too much learning he missed it. But most of all he missed the other children. He was lonesome for the other boys, the boys who now were at Boarding School. He had been with them there until a short time ago when Grandfather came to get him. How important he had felt! Being excused from Government School for a whole year to receive Zuni training!

Grandfather touched Ze-do's arm, which startled him, for he had forgotten that he was here in his Grandfather's mother's house.

Prayer was being said. Sacred cornmeal was sprinkled in the six directions. Always in the same order this sacred cornmeal was sprinkled, toward the north, the west, the south, the east, toward the sky and toward the earth. To say the directions in any other way than north, west, south, east, up and down would bring bad luck to all the people.

After the long prayers, Grandfather told Ze-do to bring the eagle. The eagle was kept in a woven willow cage on the roof of the top house by the south plaza. Ze-do ran quickly through the pueblo, across the dancing plaza and up the three ladders to the roof of the top house. He took the eagle from its cage and put it beneath his blanket. It was good to feel the eagle struggle beneath his blanket and to know that he was strong enough to keep it there.

Grandfather was pleased that his little boy had made the trip so swiftly. He smiled at him and his eyes said things that were good to know.

Uncle held the eagle's head. Another man held the eagle's feet, while Ze-do plucked its feathers. He told his fingers to be gentle and sure, for the look in his Grandfather's eyes made him want to do everything right. It took a long time to pluck the feathers that were needed, and to put each feather in the basket waiting for it. It took a long time, but he did it well. Grandfather was pleased.

After the feathers were washed, the eagle was returned to its cage on the roof of the top house by the south plaza. It was put in its cage to stay there until it was again needed for feathers.

Then the willow wands were gathered, all the same thickness, all the same size. They were brought into the house and painted. The sacred colors, black, yellow and blue were used. Each man made four prayer sticks. Ze-do made four, too. He picked out the best eagle feathers and the brightest bits of yarn to tie them to the willow wands. He made his colored bands on the willow wands straight and true. He felt happy. His heart was a little bird. He could feel it singing. It was good that Grandfather was pleased.

Grandfather explained the colors on the prayer sticks. "Black is for the dancers. Yellow is for the moon. Blue is for the sun," he told his little grandchild.

Grandfather was wise as well as good. He wanted the men to think good thoughts. So he told them stories, sacred stories.

All that night, while the men were waiting for the paint to dry on the prayer sticks, while they were waiting for the morning time to plant them, Grandfather told them stories of the days of the ancients. He told the stories to all the men, but often his hand would find Ze-do's or his eyes would smile at the little boy.

Grandfather told of the time of the angry waters and their visit to Zuni. It was one of the sacred stories. It was one of the stories of the ancients. The flood had come nearer and nearer the pueblo. At last it came in to the plazas. It melted the mud houses and washed the plants from the valley. The people were frightened. They climbed to the top of Sacred Mountain. All the old ones and all the young ones and all the mothers and the fathers climbed to the top of Sacred Mountain. The water rose higher and higher. The people could hear it screaming in anger. It came nearer and nearer to where they were on the mountain top.

At last, just as the waves were reaching their fingers in for the people, the chief gave his children to the waters. He threw his boy and his girl into the angry waters. The flood took the children in its arms and went down and down and down to the floor of the valley. There it became a river and the people went back to what was left of their houses.

Ze-do moved closer to his Grandfather. He could see the water. He could feel it cold against him. Grandfather's words came alive.

Grandfather said that the sun, moon, stars, sky, earth and water are of one family. Grandfather said that the animals are related both to the gods and to men. They are men's little brothers and they are special children to the gods.

Grandfather told the story of the clans of Zuni. He told how the people were divided into bands. Grandfather drew Ze-do close to him. It was good to sit close in the shelter of Grandfather's arm.

Grandfather said, "My son, my little Fire Child here, is one of the Badger Clan. The Badger loves the sun. In winter when Sun Father turns from his children and smiles little upon them, the Badger digs his hole in the sunny hillside. He sleeps there until the butterflies come, dragging in the warm days of summer. His home is among the roots of the juniper and the cedar whose hearts are fire."

Grandfather reached for his drum. Softly he beat it. Softly he made the singing words of the Badger song.

"On the sunny sides of hills
Burrows the Badger,
The Badger burrows
On the sunny sides of hills;
Finding and dwelling
Among the juniper,
Among the cedar
Among the dry roots
Whose hearts are fire."

"Is that why, Grandfather, that I am cross when I am cold?"

Grandfather smiled, "That is why your heart is warm," he said.

Planting Prayer Sticks

It was morning. Ze-do shivered. He could not help it; he was cold. He forgot about the Badger song. To have remembered it might have kept him warmer. He forgot about the kind ways of his Grandfather and how good it felt to do those things which pleased him. Besides being cold, Ze-do was sleepy. Besides being sleepy, he was hungry. And because of all of these the little boy was cross.

He was just as cold and just as sleepy and just as hungry and just as cross as he could be.

But all this did not matter at all. It was Zuni time for planting prayer sticks. When it is Zuni time to do anything, all the Zuni have to do it. Nobody asks the little boys if they are cold or sleepy or hungry or cross.

Grandfather picked up his prayer sticks. He wrapped his blanket tightly around him. He stood by the door. Then everybody knew that it was time to go. Everyone did just as Grandfather had done. They made a long line out into the cold grey morning.

In a long line they walked out to their frozen corn fields. In the long line walked Ze-do. With his Grandfather walked Ze-do. With the daughters and the sons of his Grandfather's mother walked Ze-do, out to the frozen corn fields.

It was cold, pushing the snow away, shoveling the frozen ground, preparing the earth to hold the winged prayers of the people. Grandfather sprinkled sacred corn-meal over the ground. He asked Sun Father to look down on the bright colored feathers standing bravely in the snow; blowing heavenward the petitions of the people. He asked Sun Father to send warmth and moisture to Earth Mother that she might bear fruit and feed the hungry.

All the others stood silent letting Grandfather and the little bright winged prayers take their hearts' thoughts up and up into the Blue-Blue above them. The bright feathers tied to the paint sticks danced and dipped in the cold winds of morning. The ends of colored yarns blew straight out like they were trying to fly. They were little feathered prayer flowers standing bravely in the snow. Again Grandfather sprinkled the prayer sticks with sacred cornmeal. With blue cornmeal he sprinkled them. With yellow and white cornmeal he sprinkled them. Again he said long prayers.

Then the Zuni were finished. They could do no more. They had planted their wing prayers to the Holders-of-the-trails-of-living.

The long line walked back to Zuni. They

walked with care, and slowly, and in silence. They had done a holy thing. They had been in touch with heaven. Their thoughts were dwelling with the All-Fathers. Their thoughts were not on earthly things.

Ze-do walked at the end. His thoughts were not on holy things. He was thinking of eating. He was thinking of bread and meat. He was thinking of Government School. There one ate and slept first and used the time that was left for doing things.

As he walked along the trail a sharp rock turned under his foot. It twisted his ankle. He stumbled and for a second blackness and pain sat heavily upon him. Then he was seeing clearly once more. The earth was right side up again. He had not fallen in the trail, nor had he cried aloud for all to hear him. Quickly he looked at the line of men in front of him. They were walking slowly and carefully. They were not talking. They were not looking backward at lit-tle boys. They had not seen him. No one ever would know that the grandson of Hotima, Sun Priest of Zuni, had dared to think of food when it was time for fasting. No one ever would know that even the rocks in the trail knew that punishment was what he needed.

Ze-do's foot hurt. Each step sent hot pain through it. But he did not limp. He did not cry. He would have been ashamed to show that punishment had come to him.

He kept on walking in the long, long line. He kept his thoughts on holy things.

When it is time for planting feathers, Zuni must plant them. Cold and lack of sleep and hunger do not matter.

The sun does not wait for anyone. The Sun Priest can not stop the count of the days.

Ze-do knew this, now. He had learned it. He would never forget it. It was his first great lesson in the ways of his people.

New Fire

Days passed at Zuni. At school the children were getting ready for Christmas. They were watching for Santa Claus. They were trimming the Christmas tree. Ze-do did not think about it. He was careful not to think about it. A dark bruise circled his ankle. It was a mark of punishment. Even the rocks in the trail knew when he failed to think as a Zuni should. He was ashamed.

Time came for the making of the New Fire. Every year all the fires of Zuni are allowed to go out; all but one, so that New Fire may be brought to every house. New Fire is the year fire for the people. It is the sacred fire of the pueblo. Only someone good may kindle it. Much thought is given to his choosing by the Council of Old Men. They must feel certain that the person is worthy.

On the morning before time for New Fire building, a runner came to the house of Hotima, Sun Priest of Zuni. The runner came in through the door so quietly and quickly it was almost like the wind coming in. The door opened. Swish, cold air came in. Grandfather looked up from his work of making moccasins. There stood the runner before him. The runner was very tall and very straight. He was very brown. He was young. Grandfather knew him. They spoke to each other.

Grandfather said, "I am making moccasins." The runner looked at them politely and answered that they were made so well that the feet they covered could not help but be swift and sure. Grandfather was pleased at this, but he replied only, "It is good buckskin."

They talked of other things, of snow and of hunting and of Navajo. That is the Indian way. To talk of other things first.

Finally Grandfather said, "A stranger does not come to the house of a stranger for nothing."

"True," said the runner, "Where is the young boy?"

He held out his hand for Grandfather to see. In it was prayer meal wrapped in cornhusk. Grandfather understood the meaning of that.

Ze-do, of all the people, had been chosen to kindle New Fire by the Council of Old Men.

When Ze-do returned, Grandfather gave him the message.

"But, Grandfather," Ze-do spoke very low. It was hard for him to talk. He had to drive his words out. They did not want to come.

"But Grandfather, I am not good. See, Grandfather. I did not want to show you, but see the bruise upon my ankle. When

my thoughts should have been on Those-Above, they were not. It was necessary that I be punished. A rock did that to me, Grandfather, I have no wisdom."

"That, my son, is wisdom—to know that you know nothing. You have been chosen, Fire Child. Go."

Ze-do followed the runner to the special house of the fire ceremony. He did all that the older men told him to do. He fasted through that day and that night, although his stomach cried out in hunger. All night he stayed in the darkness of the room alone, although his heart felt the icy fingers of witches. All Zuni was dark. There were no fires on the hearths. There were no lights in the windows. Even the stars were blotted out. There was no moon, no sound, no movement. Zuni was silent and still and black. Inside their houses the people waited for New Fire to be born. In the house of the New Fire Ze-do stayed alone. He was afraid to stay but he stayed. He was hungry, but he fasted. He did not let sleep take him into the land of not-knowing. He kept awake.

When the daylight of before-dawn turned the houses of Zuni into giant shadows, the small boy went from door to door in all the houses of the village. From each house he took the little bundles of shredded cedar bark which had been left for him. He tied them together and took the load on his back to the house of the New Fire. Then he went back for another load until all of the houses had been visited, until all the people of every house had given cedar for New Fire.

When the last load of shredded cedar bark bundles had been brought inside, Ze-do placed some of the sticks crosswise together. He made a little pen of these cross sticks and sprinkled them with sacred corn-meal. He stripped dry bark from the cedar and put it inside the little pen of cedar wood.

Then Ze-do went outside again. He went to the first house to the east and in through its open door. He found two slender forked sticks of cedar wood by the door and with them he carried coals from the fireplace there, back to the house of the New Fire. He put the coals in the little pen of crossed sticks. He knelt before them.

He blew upon the smouldering coals. He blew them into fire. He blew them into flame.

A blaze was born.

Ze-do knelt before it. He knelt on the cold earth floor before it, before the sacred New Fire.

He felt warm within. He was the Fire Child, son of the Badger people. He was needed in Zuni. The people needed him. If he were not here they would miss those things that he could do for them. Sky, earth and water and fire were part of him. He was part of the earth. They belonged to each other, these things around him. Animals were his little brothers. They spoke for him to the All-Fathers. They spoke for him to Those-Above.

Ze-do did not think of school. It dropped from him like a blanket not needed. Ze-do was Indian. Now he knew what it meant to be Indian, to be a child of the people. Now and always, as he walked the earth trails, he would feel close to he earth and close to the sky. Close to his people. All things between the earth and the sky would be brothers to him.

New Fire burned brightly for the people of Zuni.

Little Stone Wild Cat

Snow was not so deep now. On the sides of the hills and the banks of the washes small stones showed brownly against the thinning whiteness.

Ze-do had been walking among the nearby foothills. He went singing along, kicking the crusted snow up into dry, flaky cloudlets.

Now he came running back to his Grandfather's house in the plaza.

"Look, look," he cried, out of the breath with running and calling.

"Look, Grandfather, look at this small stone I found." Ze-do opened his little hand to show his Grandfather the bit of rock within it. Grandfather took the stone from the boy and held it close to his old eyes that he might see it better. He knelt by the fireplace blaze and turned it over and over. Ze-do knelt beside him, his little black head almost touching his Grandfather's hand. "Look, Grandfather. There could be the feet and tail and ears." Ze-do jumped up and down in excitement. "And right here could be a head, Grandfather. I think that way. Do you think that way, too?"

Grandfather nodded. "I think so. Yes. Come, we will go to the Chief of the Hunt." The tall old man and the little boy put their blankets on and walked across the plaza. The tall old man walked slowly with firm and steady steps for that was his way. The little boy took three big steps, just like his Grandfather, and then he forgot and made a little skip. Then he remembered and took some more big steps again, and then the little skip.

Finally they were across the plaza and in through the door of the house that belonged to the Chief of the Hunt. Ze-do hardly could wait until the two old men had talked, for the needed time, about other things. Then Grandfather opened his hand and showed the stone that Ze-do had found. The Chief of the Hunt took the stone and looked at it for a very long time, just as Grandfather had done. Ze-do had a hard time to make his feet stand still. He had a hard time to keep his hands beneath his blanket. They wanted to point out the things about the little rock. He wanted to say, "Look at this and this." But that would not have been the way to do.

At last the chief looked at him. He asked, "And what does the Grandchild think of this?" Ze-do hardly could speak. His heart was pounding like his Grandfather's drum. His voice was little. It sounded far, far away, "I think it is a wild cat. With just a little bit of my Grandfather's carving, it could be one, I think."

The Chief of the Hunt looked at Grandfather and Grandfather looked back at him. They both were pleased. The Chief said, "Yes, that is so. It has short ears." Ze-do said, "And short feet and tail." Grandfather said, "It is a wild cat."

Long time ago, when Zuni people came up through the worlds to this fourth world where they are now living, everything was mud. Everything was wet. There were big and terrible animals every place. The Sun Children tried to help the people. They sent lightning to dry the mud. When the world was dry and there was no more mud, then the animals were more terrible than ever. They could run faster and the people were afraid.

Then the Sun Children came again with their arrows of lightning. They shot the animals and turned them to stone. But their hearts they could not turn to stone. Their hearts lived on forever and forever.

And now, when the gods want to be very good to some Zuni, they let him find one of the animals that so long ago the Sun Children turned to stone. It is not often that a Zuni is so lucky as to find one but when he does, it is good.

All the way home across the plaza, Grandfather kept saying to himself, over and over and over, "It is good. It is good. It is good." He spent the rest of that day and the next and the next in carving the little animal. He kept making it better. He polished it to smooth whiteness. He put turquoise eyes in it and a turquoise in its back.

When it was finished, it had a short tail and short ears and a flat face. You could see its eyes looking. You could feel its heart living within it. It was good.

The wild cat fetish is for the south as the Badger Clan is for the south. Grandfather said that to find any kind of fetish was lucky, but to find one the same as your Clan was special.

When the little wildcat was finished Ze-do put it in a tiny fawnskin bag about his neck underneath his Zuni shirt where no one could see it and only his heart could feel it.

Ze-do whispered to it, "You pretty little wildcat of stone with turquoise eyes and living heart. You are good. You are good."

Big Fire Eater

Snow was melting fast and there was wind. Not much wind, but enough to fly the kites at school. By standing on the very top roof Ze-do could see the little boys at Day School flying their colored paper kites. Last year when Ze-do was at Boarding School he had made a big one with a long string tail.

While Ze-do was standing on the roof, his Grandfather came to the door of his house on the plaza below. He called to the boy, and Ze-do played that he was a kite coming down to the ground again. He came hopping down the ladders.

Grandfather had good news. He told his grandson that all the Zuni men were going on a rabbit hunt. Grandfather brought two rabbit sticks from the inner room, where Ze-do was never asked or allowed to go. The sticks were flat and curved. They were not long. They were made of hard wood, painted with designs and varnished with resin.

Grandfather gave Ze-do throwing lessons. When Grandfather threw the stick it always came part way back to him in a beautiful flying curve. When Ze-do threw the stick it always stayed just where he threw it. Ze-do did not like this. He liked to do things right. He tried throwing it high and he tried throwing it low, but it always

stayed where it fell. It never came part way back to him. He said, "This stick does not seem to know me." Grandfather laughed, "I have had that stick for many snows. Perhaps that is the reason it knows me and comes back to me."

When the morning of rabbit hunt was just beginning, before the sun had come, Grandfather went to the Keeper of the Fetishes. The Keeper of the Fetishes was a blind, old man, but he had taught his hands and his feet to do his seeing for him. He did not act as if he were blind. He brought all the little stone things for Grandfather to choose the one he wanted. Grandfather took the little eagle, for that is the fetish for rabbit hunts. After the blind old man had blessed the little eagle Grandfather put it next to his heart in a fawn skin bag.

Then Grandfather went back to his own house to beat the yucca suds for hair washing. No Zuni ever does a special thing, like going on a rabbit hunt, without first having washed his hair in yucca suds.

Grandfather washed his own hair. His grey hair was very thick and very long. He washed Ze-do's hair and combed it dry with the small end of his corn straw broom. Ze-do's short hair was now much longer than it had been when he came home from

school. Soon it would be long enough to do up in a chongo in the back. Ze-do laughed. He thought a chongo would be funny. Grandfather did not laugh. He said that he had told his daughter Quatsia to weave a hair tie for his little Fire Child. Ze-do stuck out his lips. He did not look at his Grandfather. He looked the other way. He said, "For me, I think, short hair is better."

Grandfather went into his inner room. This time he brought back a silver bow guard, a string of turquoise and a belt with silver conchos. Grandfather hung them on the pole-for-the-hard-things. He spoke, looking far off, as he sometimes did. "It would bring song to my heart for these to be among your possessions but, of course, having short hair, you would want only the things of short-haired people."

Grandfather went off about his business. Ze-do pulled his front hair down over his face to measure how long it was. "It would be well," he said to himself, in a small voice, "if one's hair were made of rubber bands. Then it could be short but also long, if one desired it so."

The turquoise and the silver looked at him. At least Ze-do thought they did but they did not answer.

Soon all the men gathered in the plaza to make ready to hunt the rabbits. The women stood in the house doors, and called the small children to them. Small children had to stay at home with the girls and women. Ze-do was not a small boy any longer, but he thought it well to be careful. He decided that he had time to walk down to the spring before the men started. If he were not in sight no one could tell him to stay at home.

At the spring some of the young men were riding their horses. The brave, bold ones had the young girls behind them. Ze-do thought to himself. "If I had a horse, and had more years to my age, and was brave and also bold, I, too, would have a young girl behind my saddle." He knew the young girl he would ask to ride behind him on his pony. Her name was Wai-yau-titsa. She was beautiful and good. She was smart, too, for at evening, when all the Zuni young girls went for water at the spring, all the Zuni young men smiled at Wai-yau-titsa. She never looked at any of the Zuni young men, but just walked along with her water jar upon her head. But always she would turn and smile at Ze-do and call him, "Little Brother."

It was noon before all the men were ready. Then there was much shouting and running about and wild riding of those on horseback. But at last Zuni was left behind, quiet and deserted, a town of women and children.

When the hunters reached the mesa, the men on horseback and on foot scattered to form a circle. A tree was set on fire and men passed their rabbit sticks through its flames to bring them luck in hunting. Each man took from its wrappings food which he had brought to be sacrificed in the fire of the burning tree. Some of the men remained within the circle and held fire-brands in their hands. They darted about waving the brands, making piercing, weird noises to frighten all the rabbits hiding by the pinon trees and the sage brush and the rocks and the little sand hills.

The little rabbits were frightened. They came out from their hiding places. They ran into the open space in the middle of the circle. The men with the fire-brands closed in, making the circle smaller. The men with the rabbit sticks ran after the rabbits throwing their sticks as they ran.

The circle grew smaller and smaller.

Men closed it in. Rabbit sticks went whizzing through the air. For fun, men whipped each other with yucca plants. Dust was thick. There were running horses and men and rabbits. There were flying rabbit sticks. Then Ze-do saw his rabbit. It darted by him. His blood pounded. It beat in his heart and in his ears. He gave the piercing hunting cry and threw his stick hitting the rabbit with swift sure aim. Again and again he gave the hunting cry of Zuni. The high hunting cry! The piercing hunting cry!

He was a huntsman. He liked it.

When the rabbit hunt was over, there was feasting in the pueblo. There was dancing. There was singing. There was laughter and eating. Men joked with Grandfather's Fire Boy. They called him "Big Fire Eater."

Ze-do took big steps and kept his rabbit stick beside him. He pointed his wrist where the bow guard might have been. He tied a string around his neck for turquoise beads. He tied a string around his waist and told himself it was a concho belt.

He measured his hair to see if it were long.

His Grandfather gave him a rabbit skin. "I saw you down this fellow," he told him. "I really killed one and a half," Ze-do said, " 'cause one fell down and was killed for a little while and then it got up again and ran away."

All the men thought this was very funny, but Grandfather did not laugh with them. He tied an extra tail to Ze-do's rabbitskin. He said, "That is for the half one."

Then he and his little hunter went walking off into the hills.

Baby Eagles

Snow was going from the valley. The stately old cottonwood trees were giddy girls again, flaunting the fresh new buds of spring. At dawn, when the old man and the young boy went to the edge of Zuni to watch the shadows the sun made in its journey across the sky and around the year, it was now not so cold.

Grandfather told his little son about the Rain Makers. Rain Makers are the shadow people. Their work is to gather drops of water into gourd jars from the six great waters of the world. These shadow people are so sacred that the earth people must never see them. So the gods make clouds with their breath that the Rain Makers may hide behind them. The Rain Makers pour their drops of water through these cloud masks onto the thirsty men and the thirsty fields below.

Swallows bring the rain. Zuni say, "Swallows sing for rain." Grandfather sang the swallow song for Ze-do. It is such a little song.

"Hitherward! Hitherward!
Rain clouds.
Hitherward! Hitherward!
White clouds.
He yai-e lu."

One day all the fathers of Zuni met in the plaza. They had their little boys with them. Grandfather said that they were going eagle catching. For the first time Ze-do was sorry that he was growing to be a big boy. For the first time he wished he could be little. At least, for the day of eagle catching.

All the fathers and their little boys and their grandfathers and Ze-do and his Grandfather went across the river and along the sandy trail that led up to Sacred Mountain. The fathers had coils of ropes and baskets underneath their blankets. The little boys had fast-beating hearts underneath their blankets. It takes a strong boy, and a brave one, to catch an eagle, even though it is a baby eagle.

After a long climb they reached the sharp peaks of Sacred Mountain. The great plain of Zuni looked far below them. The high houses of Zuni looked little. Ze-do remembered the blocks that the tiny children played with at school. The Zuni houses from the peaks of Sacred Mountain looked like rows of these little blocks.

Now a father was looking over the rock side. He was looking for a ledge on the cliff face for there the eagles build their nests.

All at once Ze-do gave a high cry. He was looking through a crack of rock, down, down, down. Grandfather came to stand beside him. Yes, there far below them on a

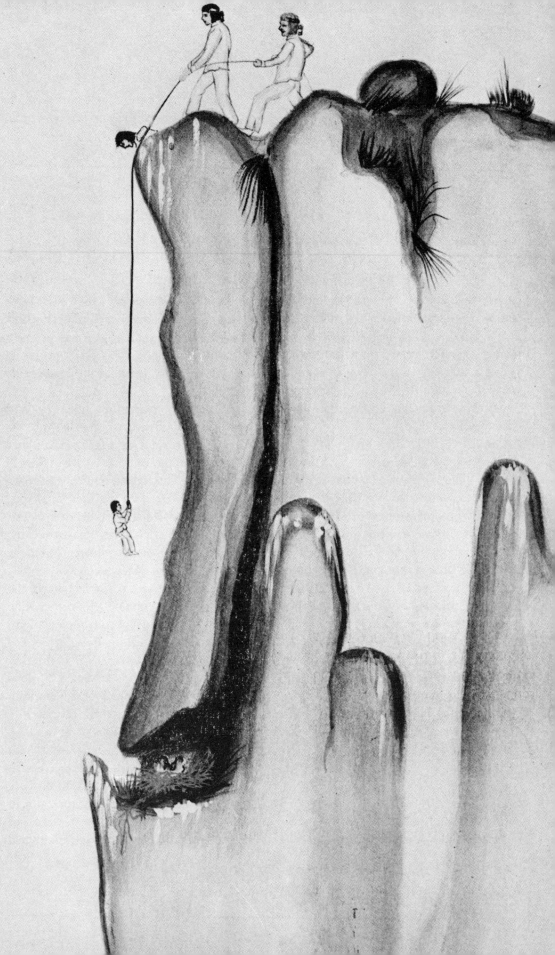

narrow shelf of rock was an eagle's nest with baby eagles in it.

The men crowded to the crack. They looked down. "Yes, yes," they said, "it is an eagle's nest." The men looked up into the blue above them. No angry mother eagle soared above her babies.

Quickly one of the men seized his little boy. Quickly he tied a rope about the child's waist, and swung him over the side of the rock cliff. Slowly, slowly, the little boy swung in a circle; his small hands held tightly to the rope going upward to his father's sure hold.

Anxiously, all the men looked down at the slowly swinging boy. Anxiously, they looked up at the empty sky. If the mother eagle should return she would attack the little boy, far down there swinging from the rope his father held.

Ze-do's breath came fast and sharp. He felt that he could not wait until the boy on the rope had captured his bird and was pulled up to safety.

At last the little boy's feet stood solidly on the rock ledge. He took his hands from the rope, and walked the few steps to the eagle nest. He looked in, then, quickly, he grabbed a baby bird and the men began to pull on the rope. Only one hand held to the rope now. The other held the eagle baby captive within his shirt.

The small body dangling from the rope end rose steadily and swiftly. Now many men were at the rope, pulling, pulling, for far, far against the sky clouds could be seen the mother eagle flying in furious flight to protect her young.

When the little boy was safely among the men again Ze-do brought the wicker cage and helped put the captive eagle in it.

He went to another rock point and searched in all crevices there and tried to be the first again to find another nest.

As each little boy went over the side of the rock cliff, Ze-do felt as if it were himself. He could feel himself swinging with the little boy, down, down, down. He could feel himself snatching the baby eagle and being pulled up, up, up, along with the little boy. Ze-do felt like the fathers when they were lowering their little boys and bringing them up again to safety.

It was a great day. Many baby eagles were captured. The fathers put the baby birds in willow cages to carry down the trail to the pueblo. The cages would be the home for the babies, now. Some of the boys insisted that they carry their own eagles down the trail. Others were glad for their fathers to help them.

Some of the old men were remembering other eagle-catching days. They were telling stories about them. Ze-do walked with them. He felt grown up, now that he was too large to do things with the little boys. He said to one of the old men, "Those children did better than I thought they could do." The old man did not even look at him as he answered, "Yes, we men forget how strong the children are."

Ze-do liked this answer very much. He said to himself, "I must say those words to my Grandfather when he and I are talking about the eagle catching."

The way home seemed very long. It was cold, too, after the sun went away. Stars lighted the sky, and candles lighted the windows of the houses of Zuni. When the men and the little boys and the captive eagles reached the plaza the house doors opened to ask them to warmth and bed. When Ze-do and Grandfather reached their house, Quatsia had fire and supper waiting for them.

Ze-do told Quatsia, "We had a fine day,

but I was never so tired before in all my life. When I eat my supper I am going to bed."

He had forgotten all about the words the old man had said to him, coming down the trail from Sacred Mountain. He had forgotten that he was going to say to his Grandfather, "We men forget how strong the children are."

Planting Time

Swallows had come with their rain song, singing:

"Hitherward! Hitherward!
Rain clouds.
Hitherward! Hitherward!
White clouds.
He yai-e lu."

And the rains came. The spring rain came. Cold and strong and life giving, it wet the fields. Everything smelled of rain. The fields, the sandy washes, the mud walls of the houses smelled of rain.

Ze-do sniffed it with long, deep breaths. He splashed with his bare, brown feet in the puddles. He scooped up handfuls of wet earth. It was good. It was clean. It had been rain washed. It felt alive and new.

Overnight, almost, little green things pushed up through the brown-crusted earth.

Overnight, almost, winter went away and spring came in its new green blanket.

The Crier told the people that it was time for planting. Because Grandfather was Sun Priest, because he had other things to do, he did not join the men to plant the fields. But he sent Ze-do. He told Quatsia's husband to take the boy into the fields. Ze-do had land of his own that had been given to him by his mother's brother.

Quatsia's husband had been to school. He talked good English. When he wanted to do so, he worked in the White man's town for money. But when he planted his fields he did them in the Zuni way. Now he said to Ze-do, "Do you know what a wash is? Ze-do did not know, but he did not want to say so. He said, "Well..." and made a line with his moccasin toe in the sand. Quatsia's husband was quick in talking. Now he said, "Well. Well what? Well you don't know what a wash is, so I will tell you. A wash is a deep, dry river bed that has water in it in the rainy season. Sometimes it has an underflow of water and that means water flowing under ground."

Ze-do was impressed. This was a grand way of talking. He liked this man who spoke the English with such an air of knowing. He looked up at him and smiled and said, softly, "Uncle how many years did you go to the school?" "Long enough to learn to give attention when my elders have things to teach me," answered Uncle and went on telling about the fields.

"We will plant your corn in these two washes. Then if one floods in the rainy season, you will still have the other crop left." "What if both flood?" Ze-do wanted to know. "You would not have any crop then. It is unlikely that both will flood because the washes are running in different directions. It would take many rains to fill all the different running washes. But I think that neither one will flood."

After the place for the fields had been chosen, Uncle taught Ze-do how to make a dam across the wash with logs and dirt and weeds. Uncle explained why a dam was needed. When the rain waters come, this way they would hit the dam and spread out. That would water the fields instead of flooding them with a single stream. It took several days to finish the dams, although other men came to help them. Then Uncle and Ze-do cleared the ground and brushed it. They marked the boundary line and put large stones at the corners. They built sage-brush fences to act as windbreaks when the new corn came up, weak and tender.

By this time the fields were ready to be blessed. Grandfather brought the Corn Priest who blessed the ground and prayed for fruitful crops. Grandfather gave Ze-do his own planting stick which was smooth as polished bone from many years of using. "It belonged to my grandfather's father, and his father before him. Take it, my son, use it and hand it down to your sons and the sons of your sons."

Time for planting came. In the middle of the field Uncle dug a hole with his planting stick. He showed Ze-do how large and how deep to make the hole. Uncle gave the ceremonial seeds to Ze-do. To the north they planted yellow corn kernels, to the west blue, to the south red, and to the east they planted white corn kernels. They planted mixed corn for the sky and black corn for the earth. Then they planted the rest of the field with the colored corn which belonged to the different parts of it.

It was hard work. When all the field was planted, Ze-do said, "Now we can rest until the corn is ready to be eaten." But Uncle said, "Indeed, you cannot rest. Now you can work to make sure that the corn will grow big enough to be eaten."

He explained how all through the growing season they must keep the weeds from choking the little corn sprouts. They must look at each green leaf to find the cutworms hiding there. They must make snares to catch the chipmunks and the prairie dogs, and scarecrows to frighten off the thieving birds. After every sand storm they must brush with their hands the loose sand from around the new green leaves. They must build little weed shelters to protect each baby corn stalk against the too playful winds. They must pray for rain. They must dance for rain. They must shake the rattle and pound the drum and beat the earth floor with their feet for rain.

Rain. Rain. Drink for the corn plants. Water for the fields. Life for the people. Hitherward. He yai-e lu. Ze-do went each morning to each little mound of earth that held deep and warm within it the precious seeds of baby corn. He said to Uncle, "This earth is so good. Just think of all the things it gives us." Uncle nodded, "Yes and the sun and the rain are also good. All things are friends to the people."

Grandfather came walking over the little hill. He came to say the rain prayer with Uncle and this small boy who was so dear to him.

"May the Rain Makers water Earth
    Mother
    that she may become beautiful to look
    upon.
May the Rain Makers water Earth
    Mother
    that she may give to her children
    and to all the world
    food,
    that they may have food
    so that the children of the world
    may live the span of life
    and then sleep
    to awaken with their gods."

Stick Race

After planting was finished the Crier told the people to get ready for the stick race.

Ze-do could run as swiftly as a young deer. At school he had been known as the fastest of the small boys. Although he was very young, the people of the south plaza chose him as a member on the team for their side. Grandfather was a little worried. He was afraid that Ze-do was too young to be able to run fast enough. The other men told him not to worry. They said, "That one is fast enough. Besides he is a favored one of the gods. Did he not make the New Fire? Did he not find a hunting fetish? Did he not kill his first rabbit with the first swing of his rabbit stick?"

Grandfather felt a little better when the men had finished talking to him. All that they had said was true.

In Zuni there are several kinds of stick races during the year. There are the ceremonial races to bring rain to the crops of the fields and the fun races. This stick race was for fun and young men, only, were in it. In the ceremonial races in which Grandfather and Uncle ran, the course was often twenty-five miles, but this one was much shorter.

There were to be but three men on each side and the south plaza was matched against the north plaza.

For many days before the race the runners practiced. Grandfather would let no one train Ze-do but himself. All day long Ze-do thought of the race. Every morning and every evening he practiced running. He ran up hill and he ran down hill, he ran through arroyos and across the river. He ran slowly and for long distances. Sometimes he ran as swiftly as the wind through the valley.

He became lean and hard. His muscles rippled like water tumbling over stones. He seemed to have grown taller. All his movements became sure and steady as if he were listening to music. Perhaps he was for his heart was singing within him.

The people were betting on the stick race. They bet horses and sheep and saddles and wagons. They bet silver and turquoise. They bet bracelets and rings and necklaces. They bet pottery and blankets and baskets.

On the evening before the day of the race, the runners went up to the mesa. There they prayed until nightfall for swiftness and for strength.

On the way back they watched for omens. If an owl had hooted or if a sleeping bird had wakened and taken flight, or if a star had fallen, the omen would have been bad. When they returned Grandfather

asked Ze-do about these things. Ze-do told him, "No bird cried out or flew away in fright. No star fell. All was still." As Ze-do spoke, Grandfather's parrot, sleeping on his perch stirred drowsily. A bright green feather fluttered lazily downward and rested lightly on Ze-do's black hair.

For a second Grandfather stood speechless, he was so surprised and so delighted. In Zuni, at the Sun Priest's house, there is always a parrot though often it means a many months' journey into Mexico on a trading expedition to get it. A parrot is prized for its feathers which are used ceremoniously.

And now to have the parrot give one of his sacred feathers to Ze-do was a better omen than even Grandfather could have wished for.

He took the concho belt and the bow guard and the turquoise necklace from where they were hanging on the pole-for-the-hard-things. He said that he was going to bet them. He said, "All Indians like to bet; not just our people here in Zuni, but Indians everywhere. We bet on horse racing and foot racing and tug-of-war. We have betting games. We even have betting dances."

Grandfather chuckled. He told Ze-do at the last betting dance at Zuni he had lost a saddle. He said that John's son had stood on the highest house in Zuni dressed as a Comanche dancer. The people stood in the plaza watching him. Grandfather had bet it was Natchi of the Tobacco Clan people. Grandfather said, "I should not have trusted my eyes on that day. It was an unlucky day for me."

Grandfather chuckled again. "I am glad I am going to get that saddle back again," he said, as he went out the door swinging the concho belt, the bow guard and the necklace.

Ze-do stood in the door watching his Grandfather as long as he could see him. "Grandfather is going to bet that belt and necklace and that bow guard," he said to himself. Then he sat himself on the floor under the parrot perch. For a long time he sat there. He was hoping for another falling feather. He felt that it might be well to have another good omen.

After sunrise the next morning, the trail was sprinkled with cornmeal. Prayers were said. The runners and their sticks were blessed. Everything was made ready.

The stick belonging to the south plaza was as large as man's finger. It had a center band of red. The north plaza stick was like it except it had two end bands of red.

A Bow Priest pointed out the directions that the runners were to take. Then he sprinkled cornmeal four times. The fourth time was the sign to "Go."

The race began. Ze-do was first to kick the stick for his side. He caught it between his toes and sent it up a little way and forward a long way; at the same time someone else kicked the stick for the other side. Fast and furious the race was on. Everyone watched the stick as it flew through the air. Everyone tried to be where it would fall so that he would be the one to kick it forward on its way again. Only once did Ze-do become so tired that he lagged behind; only once and for a very little time, and a very little way. Then he was up front again running, dodging in between his team mates, watching the stick and kicking it when he could get to it first.

The racing trail led through the fields, the foothills, the arroyos and the river. It circled the pueblo. Some places it is narrow and rocky. At other places there is deep sand that tries to hold the runner's feet.

Again and again they had to cross the river. They had to run through the water and kick the stick to the other side. Some of the trail was bordered with pinon and sagebrush. Not once did Ze-do's side kick the stick among the shrubs where it was hard to find. One time someone had kicked it in some cactus, but Ze-do was there to kick it out lightly with his toes. And if he got thorns in his toes, who would know? A race is to be won!

All the people of the pueblo went with the runners. Many were riding their horses. There was much laughter and fun-making. The horsemen rode fast and hard and kept circling the runners. They made shrill and piercing cries and Zuni calls. They were waving yards and yards of bright-colored calicos for streamers and banners.

On and on ran the racers. Whenever it was Ze-do's chance to kick the stick, he sent it up and far. When someone else was kicking it, he watched the stick go flying through the air. He tried to be just where the stick would be when it came down to earth again.

On and on they ran and stopped to kick the stick and then ran on again. Up the hills, through the arroyos and across the river went the runners sweating and panting.

On and on came all the people shouting and waving their streamers of calico. Flashing by and turning back and circling were the horses and their riders. The people called to the runners, urging them on with the noise of their voices, speeding them on with the haste of their own actions.

On and on around the fields and the pueblo raced the runners of the south plaza and the north plaza. They had started at the south. Now they ran from south to east, crossing the river and on toward the north, keeping to the foothills, and crossing the river again, and again to the west and then south and back to the starting place.

Ze-do's last kick sent the stick whizzing across the line, and into the river.

The race was finished! Ze-do's side had won it!

The men yelled and shouted. The women laughed and called to each other. The dogs barked and ran around in circles.

Grandfather said it was a good day for him because his grandson had helped his clansmen win their bets.

In the center of the plaza were piled the possessions of the people. They were the things that they had bet. There were saddles and blankets and bridles and baskets. There was corn and silver and turquoise and coral and shell. Around them were the horses and the wagons. Everyone remembered what he had bet and with whom he had bet.

It did not take Grandfather long to bring back all his new possessions and all his old possessions because he had won his bets. He brought back the turquoise and the belt and the bow guard among many other things. He brought back, also, a hair tie which he had told Quatsia to weave for him.

Ze-do was glad to see the things that belonged there back in place on the pole-for-the-hard-things. He felt relieved.

He said, "I am glad that I did all the things that I should have done in the stick race. Grandfather, have you noticed how much my hair is growing?"

Grandfather acted surprised to see how long his hair was. He did it up in a chongo. It was a very little thin chongo, but Grandfather seemed to like it.

"Now that you are one of the long-haired people, perhaps you might like to have this bow guard?"

Ze-do's heart leaped with joy, but of course he had to be polite. To show too much haste or too great desire would not be the thing to do. Grandfather would not like it. So, Ze-do said, "Yes, perhaps I should like it. Is it a good one?"

Grandfather answered that the guard was good and so were the belt and the string of turquoise.

When Ze-do walked again, among his clansmen in the plaza, he had a chongo, a woven hair tie, a bow guard, a string of turquoise and a concho belt of silver.

Truly life was good.

Uncle Goes to the Salt Lakes

After planting time, after the stick race, came the time for the yearly trip to the Salt Lakes. The Salt Lakes lie to the south of Zuni. They are sacred. The salt which their waters hold is precious. There is but one time during the year when salt is taken from the Salt Lakes. Only the runners go, and the drivers of the pack burros. Grandfather was not to be among them. He was needed at home.

When Ze-do asked if he could go to the Salt Lakes, his Grandfather gave much thinking before he answered. Into the night he sat smoking and thinking and looking into the burning wood in his fire place. Ze-do unrolled his blankets and made his bed on the floor as he always did. He lay down on the blankets with his back toward his Grandfather. It would not be well to let his eyes tell the Grandfather how much he wanted to go. It is not well to let the heart tell its own secrets.

It grew colder and outside were the night noises of the pueblo. The fireplace wood burned brightly and noisily and sent out lazy puffs of blue cedar smoke to sting shut tired eyes. Ze-do slept.

The night grew colder.

He wakened when it was time to go for the morning sun prayer. Grandfather told no stories on the way to the edge of the village. Soft clouds hung over Zuni, washing with night rain the faces of the sand dunes. Ze-do thought of the Rain Makers hiding behind the cloud masks. He let his heart whisper the words of the rain-prayer.

The sun rose, red and gold, and colored the cloud masks with its fire. Grandfather noted the sun shadow and turned toward Zuni. Then he spoke to his small boy. He said, "The way to the Salt Lakes is long. It is a sacred journey. Those who are chosen to go will taste the salt of tears on their lips before they have finished. It is too hard a thing that you ask to do. Wait until you have more years for such an undertaking."

"But, Grandfather." Grandfather pulled his blanket over his face. Only his eyes showed and they looked cold and black like the jet in Quatsia's necklace. There was no talking. There were no sounds, only the pat, pat of the two pairs of moccasins on the wet sands of the home trail.

When they reached home they learned that Quatsia's husband was among those who had been chosen to go to the Salt Lakes. Ze-do did not like this. He went over to Quatsia's house and stood around, looking at Quatsia's husband. He said, "I am almost as big as you are." Quatsia's husband laughed at him. "Almost half as big, you mean," he answered.

The runners to the Salt Lakes were gone for five days. Ze-do thought those days would never end. He pretended that he had gone with them. He pretended that he was running, running, running to the Salt Lakes. "Now we are going through the sand. We are running through the sand. The sand is deep. It is heavy. It pulls our feet," he would say to himself. And, "I am very thirsty. I have had no water. I am hungry. I have had no food." He shut his eyes and he could feel himself running, running, running to the Salt Lakes.

On the fifth day the runners returned. It would take many more days before the drivers of the pack burros would bring the bags of salt into the plaza.

After the people of Zuni had received the runners, Quatsia's husband sat in the shade of his house door. His face looked thin. His eyes looked tired. Ze-do sat beside him. He could see those runners on their sacred journey. They had eaten but little food and moistened their mouths with but drops of water. They had run slowly, at the same pace, at the same distance from each other. They kept their heads down,

looking only at the ground beneath their jogging feet. Sweat rolled down their faces and into their eyes, making them sting and water. Dust rose from the trail and thickened their breathing. The sun burned hot, parching their throats, blistering the soles of their feet. Heat haze made the far line of earth and sky dance dizzily. And the way was long, so long, so very long.

Ze-do sighed. Perhaps he had been small for such an undertaking. He put his hand in the thin brown one of Quatsia's husband. Perhaps it was better to wait until he was larger and stronger. It would have been a terrible thing to start that which one could not finish. He whispered, "My Uncle, does it not seem strange to you that the Grandfather always knows best?" Uncle smiled, "He always does. That is his way," he answered.

Ze-do put his feet straight out in front of him. He leaned his head back against his Uncle's shoulder. He closed hs eyes against the light. White clouds filled his mind empty of thinking.

He and his Uncle were resting. The journey to the Salt Lakes was finished.

Summer Solstice

Days grew long. Sun Father shone down hot and bright on his brown-skinned children. Zuni world was filled with dazzling white light, misted with lazy dust clouds and smoky heat haze. Wild flowers bloomed in the sandy washes. The fields were green with new corn growing.

Sun Father came earlier and earlier in the mornings and stayed later and later every evening. It was as though he did not want to go away because Zuni was quietly happy and so brightly warm.

Ze-do liked, now, to get up to greet the sun with prayer and sacred offering. He did not remember the cold, snow-filled dawns when he had stumbled and grumbled behind his tall, fast-walking Grandfather. Now, he walked beside the tall old man. Now, he looked around him as he walked along. The air was washed with summer nightdamp and it smelled clean and fresh. Little growing things bowed to each other and to him and danced in the little sunrise breeze. "Before the day gets all waked up, it's awfully nice, isn't it, Grandfather?"

Grandfather was thinking of other things. He did not hear him. But the little flowers heard Ze-do and nodded their bright-colored heads. A bluebird heard Ze-do and looked at him from the mesquite bush. A prairie dog stuck his fat, little head out of the door of his house and wrinkled his nose at Ze-do. "They all know me because I am with Grandfather," thought the little boy. "Perhaps they think that I am helping him to count the days for the people."

On this morning sunrise seemed more beautiful than ever before. It was so big, so very red, so grand and powerful. It was so beautiful, wrapped in its clouds of pink and blue and purple and grey and lavender. At first the clouds had huddled together for Sun Father to bless them with color and then they had spread out over the whole sky and had sprinkled those colors on the sand world below them.

Ze-do stood still beside his Grandfather while the old man prayed for the world, for the new day and for his people. Suddenly, to the little boy, it seemed that the old man changed. He looked different. He was not just Grandfather. He was Zuni Sun Priest. He was Sun Father's messenger. He stood between the beautiful, sacred sun and the people. Ze-do felt a little strange and in awe of this tall man whom the sun had chosen and blessed. He felt a little lonely as if never again could he come quite close to this man who held in his keeping the days for his people.

45

Then Grandfather smiled at him and everything was all right again. He was the Grandfather, kind and understanding, as always. He was the Grandfather who talked to his little boy, who fed him when he was hungry and made him warm when he was cold.

Ze-do reached under Grandfather's blanket and found the kind, strong hand and held it tight. He pushed close to the rough worn blanket and smiled into the friendly eyes looking down at him.

Grandfather was explaining Summer Solstice. "When Sun Father moves to the north, when he passes the gentle Moon Mother, he will continue round to yonder point northwest of Zuni." Grandfather pointed. "Note well that point between the sky world and the valley; that point which is called Great Mountain. Do you see it?"

Ze-do looked. He saw Great Mountain, as Grandfather had described it, between the sky world and the valley. It seemed to be a holding-place where the blue of the sky and the blue of the world came together.

"When the sun touches this place at evening time he finds it so perfect that again and again at the close of the day he comes back to it," Grandfather said. "Nowhere else in his daily journey over the world does he ever stop a second day at the same place."

Now Grandfather and his little helper went evenings as well as mornings to observe the sun, his acts and his shadows. Ze-do found it hard to wait until the evening ball of fire should come to rest on yonder point above Great Mountain.

But at last, one late afternoon, as the tall old man and the little boy watched the sun slip across the sky to the twilight line, it happened. The red ball of fire found the point above Great Mountain, and the clouds made a cup to hold it there.

Grandfather finished his prayer. He finished the evening ceremony of his petition to Sun Father for his children, the Zuni. He and Ze-do returned to the pueblo to tell the Priest of the Bow and the Priest of Rain that Summer Solstice was beginning and they should go in retreat to pray.

The next morning Grandfather made prayer sticks to Sun Father and to Moon Mother, and he planted them at sunset time before the shrine to the sun.

One, two, three, four, five evenings Sun Father rested above the point of Great Mountain, and Grandfather, Sun Priest of Zuni, was then ready to tell the people that he knew by that sign the half year of Winter Solstice was finished, and the half year of Summer Solstice was coming to take its place.

Then the people fasted and prayed. There were night prayers and songs accompanied by the pattering-rain music of rattles. There was no drum to break the silvery flow of singing. There was no movement except the swift, light skill of reverent fingers fashioning prayers of feathers.

At dawn the prayer sticks were finished, and the people greet Sun Father's coming with the song of flutes. They went in long lines to their fields and planted the fluffy bits of colors coaxing Sun Father's favor on the people of the land.

For the next three days all of Zuni stirred with activity. Women molded and painted pottery jars all day. And all night they fired them, giving to each pot a bit of bread that its spirit might not be hungry; that the spirit of the bread might feed and make strong the spirit of the pot.

Different bands of people went to different springs taking prayer offerings to the waters within them to beg the gifts of summer rain. As Ze-do stood beside the Sun Priest and saw the men go into the waters, saw them dip their bowls and lift them skyward, saw them sacrifice their offerings, and breathe the prayers, he understood the oneness of earth and sky and water and men. He did not know that such understanding was born within him. He could not have said it with words, but he knew it. For every moment of his life henceforth he would be serenely conscious of the scheme of natural things.

Summer Solstice ceremonies went on and on under the gathering white heat of summer days, under the low hanging clouds of summer nights.

On the last days, those who had been chosen at Winter Solstice as the impersonators of the Shalako gods for the coming end of the Zuni year, went on their summer pilgrimage to the Mother Spring.

Only those who had been chosen to be the holy impersonators went. They were led out of the village by the Sun Priest, and Ze-do was among them.

The world about the Zuni great plain lay hushed in morning sunlight; lay bathed in white sunlight and summer stillness. Dust clouds rose, hiding the figures of the men on the way to Mother Spring, and fell softly after them, hiding their footsteps.

What happened on the pilgrimage only those who have been so chosen must ever know but when they returned one midnight they were led by the young Ze-do carrying a lighted fire-brand.

And Zuni woke up the next morning and went about its tasks of every day.

Every-day tasks at Zuni were as a blanket covering Zuni living.

New Learning

No rain came to wet the sun-baked land. The little growing things drooped with thirst. The little winds panted with hot, dry breath. Whirlwinds danced like enemy warriors, glad that no rain fell to heal the heat-wounded earth.

Ze-do drooped, too, like the wild flowers and the young corn. His skin felt dry and harsh. He felt dry and harsh inside.

Grandfather told him to bring water from the river to Quatisa's garden. Ze-do did not like it. He did not want to bring water to the women's gardens. He went the longest way round and made slow dragging steps through the white dust on the road to the river.

The women's gardens are on the south edge of the pueblo. They look like waffles with new shoots of green growing in each little square. In them the women grow onions and chili and herbs for seasonings. Only the children are sent to bring water to the women's gardens. Ze-do felt that he, Ze-do, should be above such work. He stopped to trace a snake track in the sand by the sage brush. A lazy lizard was sitting in the sun. Ze-do told him, "I am not pleased about this bringing water to the women's gardens." The lazy lizard slid off the sunny rock and slipped away through the cactus.

Ze-do watched a puff cloud rolling high above Sacred Mountain. He knew what lay behind that puff cloud. "And to think," he grumbled, "that I, who know so many things, am sent to carry water to the women's gardens."

Ze-do took a long time to fill his water jar and walk back with it up the trail from the river. Other boys, now home from Government School, were running up and down the trail between the river and the gardens.

They liked the work of bringing water. They shouted and ran and jumped and called to each other. They wanted to talk with Ze-do. They said to him, "You sure missed it up at that school." They said, "Now you are behind in books. We will be in fifth grade."

Ze-do did not answer such small boys, taking water to their mothers' gardens.

At last he reached Quatsia's garden. Quatsia was not there, but Grandfather was there. Ze-do began to hurry. His Grandfather watched him coming. Ze-do looked at the little squares of garden. The new green shoots were standing in water. Grandfather looked at Ze-do. "I brought the water, son, since the task was not to your liking."

Grandfather walked away. He walked

toward the mesa. His blanket flapped out behind him. It looked angry. Ze-do watched him walking. He had made his Grandfather do small boy's work! Slowly he poured out the water from his water jug. It made a round dark hole in the dry sand. A lizard slipped by his hand. Ze-do's eyes darkened. He had seen that lizard before. This morning on his way to the river, he had seen that lizard. "Oh, so you told on me, did you?" he said, very low, to the lizard.

Ze-do hid Quatsia's water jug in its hiding place. Ze-do's ears burned. He knew what they were saying. They were talking about him. They were saying that he had made his Grandfather do small boy's work.

Ze-do sat under the cottonwood tree and hid his face in his blanket.

That he should do that to his Grandfather.

Sun Father burned hot on his shoulders.

Far away he could hear the school boys laughing. They were swimming in the river. Ze-do kept his face in the folds of his blanket. By and by tears squeezed out of his tight shut eyes and rolled slowly down his cheeks, making two little rivers in the dusty brown face. By and by his head nodded and dropped down to the soft sand beneath the cottonwood tree. Tears stopped. The boy slept.

The puff clouds in the sky gathered together, closer and closer, like sheep before shearing. Whirlwinds danced faster on the edges of the far places. A wind came, bringing a wet smell. Sun Father hid behind the masks of the Rain Makers.

Slowly it began to rain. Soft little drops of water, teasing little drops of water playing and spattering. Drop, drop, drop. Getting bigger. Getting closer together. Getting faster and faster.

Rain. Rain.

Ze-do woke up. He stretched out his hands to the warm summer wetness. He took off his blanket. He took off his moccasins. He took off his shirt. The pelting raindrops felt good against him. He began to sing. He began to dance. He heard the school boys shouting and laughing on the banks of the river. He ran to where they were. He joined them in their singing and shouting and laughing and dancing because it was raining. Because it was raining and rain feels good to growing boys and growing corn.

After awhile the rain stopped. It had been just a little rain, enough to wet the thirsty plants and wash the faces of the sand dunes. Before long it would be dry again. By tomorrow the plants would be thirsty again. Ze-do ran to the door of Quatsia's house. He stuck his brown face around the corner of the fireplace wall and rolled his black eyes and flashed his white teeth at Quatsia. "Would you let me water your garden all the days that it does not rain?" he wanted to know. Quatsia smiled at him and nodded. "Because," said Ze-do, "watering the women's gardens is hard work for women. It takes boys as big as I am to do it."

Grandfather came home from walking. He did the things he had to do. He acted as he always did, quiet and kind and happy, deep within himself. At first, Ze-do was a little uneasy. He was afraid his being cross might have taken shape and come to stand between him and his dear Grandfather. But as twilight slid into darkness he felt all right again. Grandfather showed him, without words, that everything was all well again between them.

As soft, grey dusk blanketed the yellow light of day, Grandfather went to sit before

his open door. Ze-do squatted down beside him, and together they watched the happenings of Zuni evening.

A little wind was herding the left-over clouds together for night camp. Grandfather explained about winds and clouds. He told Ze-do that the southeastern and the southwestern winds are summer winds. They are the little breaths from the hearts of the Rain Makers. Grandfather said never to fear lightning for it did not destroy those who were good in heart. He said that the cirrus clouds were made by the Rain Makers, playing and running about in their sky home, but when there are cumulus and nimbus clouds overhead it is a sign that the Rain Makers are getting ready to wash the earth.

Grandfather said there are two kinds of rain. One is made by the Rain Makers sprinkling the earth gently by dipping prayer plumes in gourds of water. When they make the other kind of rain they pour the contents of their gourds directly on the land below.

Grandfather was very talkative. It seemed as if he had so much to say that he would never finish in just one night.

He drew the sleepy Ze-do to him. "Sun Father and Moon Mother and Rain Makers help us, but we, in turn, must help our weaker brothers. Corn must have water or it dies. And we must have corn or we hunger, and to hunger is to die."

Stars hung lower and lower. Ze-do slept against his Grandfather's arm. The old man raised his eyes skyward and softly breathed his night prayer.

"We pray that all things will help our people, and all the people of the world, that they may not die, but sleep to awaken."

Harvest

The Boarding School children went back to school. Some had new paper-backed suitcases or bright tin trunks. Others had to be content for another year with having their belongings tied up in a flour sack. Everyone had bundles of Zuni bread and strings of dried meat pieces.

Ze-do watched the children go. Many of them cried when the school bus came, but there was an undercurrent of excitement. Even the youngest knew that in a few days they would feel as if they had always been at school. Even the youngest knew that school had its advantages. At school there was always enough food, and school was warm in winter.

Ze-do stood close to his Grandfather. He was needed in Zuni. His Grandfather needed him. The people needed him. It felt good to be so needed that you could not be spared.

Days came and went in Zuni.

The sun set earlier now as if he were hurrying somewhere else. As if he had to make up time for his long rest at the point above Great Mountain. The wind had a little sting, now, when it brushed by Ze-do's cheek or tugged at the corners of his blanket. One night the first frost came in gleaming patches of silver crystals.

Grandfather said it was time to harvest.

He and Ze-do went to Quatsia's house to help Quatsia and her husband and her children. They must make ready for winter.

There was threshing of wheat and of beans. Ze-do helped drive the horses round and round the threshing ring. It was great fun driving the horses round and round so that their sharp hoofs would push the little beans out from their green blankets. All the boys ran and ran after the horses to keep them moving. All the boys shouted and shouted to hurry them along. When Ze-do could run no more he leaned against the bars of the threshing ring fence and still kept shouting. And when he could shout no more he lay down in the sand wash near by with the other boys and watched the men run the horses round and round over the beans.

Ze-do helped Uncle bring in the corn when it was ready. They brought it in from the fields and piled it high before Quatsia's door because now it belonged to her.

Then Ze-do brought in his own small harvest of corn ears. He put it before Grandfather's door. The pile was not nearly so high as Uncle's corn. "Perhaps if I had chased more rabbits and gophers; perhaps if I had hoed it better, it would now be higher," Ze-do said to himself.

When Grandfather saw Ze-do's corn harvest he was very pleased. And all at once the pile seemed much higher than it had seemed, and all the corn ears in it looked almost perfect.

Grandfather picked out a yellow corn ear, a blue one, a red one, a white one, one that was mixed colored, and a black corn ear. He placed the different colored corn side by side and ran his wrinkled old hand lovingly over them. Ze-do ran his slender hand over them, too, just as Grandfather had done. "Don't you think it would be well if in all things I could be just like you, Grandfather?" he asked. Into the old man's eyes came a far away look. "Wait and see what tomorrow brings forth," was all that he answered. Ze-do did not think much of that answer. It was an old man's saying. Tomorrow and tomorrow would always be like now.

That was what Ze-do thought.

All the people at Quatsia's house were working hard. Besides the wheat and corn and beans to be made ready for winter there was chili. Chili to tie in long scarlet strings and hang on the outside walls of the houses to dry. There were melons to cut into strips and hang on the drying lines. Ze-do laughed at the Zuni word for melons. It means little-round-sit-downs.

For five days they camped at the peach orchard at the foot of Sacred Mountain. The peach trees there are so little, so twisted, so scrubby. Many of them are only three feet high, but the peaches are sweet and juicy.

Days at the peach orchard are happy days. All day the children not old enough to got to school, pick and eat peaches. Old people pick them and put them in bags to take back to their homes.

When the children grow tired of picking peaches, they catch grasshoppers for the eagles in the willow cages on the housetops of Zuni. They catch them with a tassel of weeds tied to a long stick.

The men who have been to school make jokes. They say the boys are going grasshopper-fishing. The old men make jokes too. They say the grasshoppers are going to visit the eagles.

At night all the families make camp near their own trees. They untie their bed rolls and make their own small cooking fires. After everyone has eaten and the fires are burning low, the small boys play. They run dancing about with fire brands. Old men sing softly. The boys with their flaming torches, the stars and the smoldering camp fires dot the foot of Sacred Mountain with little flecks of burning light.

Finally everyone sleeps and only the stars look down at the people camping by their peach trees in the old, old orchard at the foot of Sacred Mountain.

When camping is over, the peaches are brought back to the houses. There they are cut in half and the seeds are taken out. Then they are placed on squares of canvas or worn-out blankets on some sunny housetop to dry in the sun.

The store room in each house is bright with color and smells dry and sweet with the sun-ripened foods put away there for winter. Hanging from the vigas are the seed corn of many colors, the strings of scarlet chili, the yellow half moons of melons. There are also gay little bunches of herbs from the women's gardens, and onions and beans. On the floor are piles of yellow wheat and piles of colored corn and little mounds of shriveled peaches.

Ze-do felt proud of his own corner in his Grandfather's store room where corn from his own field made its own little pile. Corn that he had planted, that he had watered and cared for and tended was now to serve him against the hunger of winter: corn that was to make him stronger and bigger and perhaps more brave to meet the happenings along the trail.

Sitting in the quiet, sweet-smelling storeroom, Ze-do suddenly felt wiser. He felt that he understood what his Grandfather was trying to teach him. The Sun Father gave warmth to the earth; the Rain Makers gave water to the earth, and the earth gave corn to the people that they might live. The corn pile beneath his hand was life. Gift of the Sun Father and the Earth Mother, nourished by rain, it held the spirit of the living for the people.

Gathering the Wild Plants

After the things of the fields and gardens are put away in the store rooms for winter, the people gather the wild plants. Zuni try to keep a year's supply of food ahead so that hunger can not catch them unprepared.

Grandfather told Ze-do that Earth Mother had given the plants of the world to the Star People while they were still living on earth, before they were gone to their sky home. Grandfather said it had been the Star People who had scattered the plant seeds near where people were to live.

He said that wild ducks had been sent to fly low over the new corn plants. Their spreading wings protected the little plants while they were growing.

Ze-do learned the times of day. He learned to call sunrise the sun-come-out-time. Noon is sun-at-middle. Sunset is sun-sitting. Evening is known as yellow-lost.

Ze-do learned about wild plants.

He learned that jack rabbits drink the milk of the milk weed.

He learned that thistle is made into perfume and that its roots are good for chewing gum.

Many plants are good for medicine, like the red willow, pinon and thistle. But plants that are used for medicines belong to certain people and not to everyone. The secret of their use sells high. "For money?" asked Ze-do. "Yes, for money or some other things, perhaps, which have greater value than money." Ze-do said that he thought money was the greatest of all things. Grandfather said, "If you were lost in a snow storm, which would you rather have, a buckskin bag of money or fire and shelter?" Ze-do thought a long time. "I would rather have a horse, Grandfather." His Grandfather laughed. He answered, "Everyone should have a horse. You, too, some day will have one, but today there is other work to do. We must help prepare the yucca.

"Yucca is a good plant. It has many uses. Its fibers are made into brushes for painting pottery. Its leaves are boiled and crushed and made into string. The stems are knotted into rope. Woven baskets and mats may be plaited of yucca, but very few Zuni do this any more."

"Why don't all the people weave baskets now, Grandfather?" Ze-do asked.

"They have forgotten how to do so. Wisdom not used becomes blunt, as a knife left too long in its covering of deerskin," Grandfather answered sadly.

Then Quatsia called them to come watch Uncle help the women make yucca

fruit rolls. Quatsia thought it was very funny that the women were making Uncle work. Uncle thought it was funny, too. He laughed and teased them while he helped them boil the fruit and crush its pulp into round rolls. When the yucca fruit rolls were made it was Uncle who hid them away in the house walls. Grandfather told Ze-do that, although the children saw where Uncle hid the rolls, they would not touch them. Grandfather said very loud. "To hide a thing is the same as locking it away. To hide a thing means that the owner does not want it touched." All the little children looked at Grandfather when he said this. Their eyes were very big and round and black. Uncle said to Ze-do, "And anyway, they know that in winter the fruit rolls taste twice as sweet as they do while they are being made." Uncle said this in English. Uncle laughed when he said it. Ze-do laughed too, a little. He picked up some yucca roots lying on the ground. Quatsia told him to take them to Grandfather's store-room. "When you need them you can pound them up. The pounded roots make good soap."

Grandfather wanted Ze-do to help with everything. Wherever there was a group working together he and Ze-do went among them. "It is good to know what the people are doing. I want you to know many things, Grandchild. Great wisdom is made of the complete knowledge of little happenings."

Ze-do helped gather wild tobacco. He helped boil the purple bee-plant into paste. Quatsia taught him how to wrap it in corn husks and tie the little fat bundles in a chain together. Bee-plant paste makes black paint for pottery. Bunches of the flowers and leaves are dried and afterward cooked with corn and chili.

Ze-do went with Uncle to the Zuni mountains to gather the bark of alder to dye deerskin reddish brown. They gathered Indian paint brush, too. The Zuni name for this flower is hummingbird-food. It is used with a kind of rock to dye deerskin black.

Ze-do went with the rest of the small boys to gather ko-shi fruit. Ko-shi is cactus. The boys had great fun running and shouting, while they gathered the ko-shi. If anyone was so clumsy as to get a ko-shi thorn instead of ko-shi fruit all the other boys shouted and pointed. Everyone always gets at least one thorn. Ze-do tried to hide his hand when he got a thorn, but all the boys knew and they cried, "Ho O. Ho O."

Ko-shi fruit is the best kind. It is better, even, than peaches. What the children could not eat they were willing to bring home to their mothers to eat. Ze-do brought his to Grandfather. The next day he went with Quatsia to help her gather some ko-shi fruit. She showed him how to pick it with split sticks to keep from getting thorns. They worked swiftly. Before very long they had a basket full.

After they got back to Quatsia's house she cleaned the fruit of its little thorns. Then when it was dried and pounded she would mix it with wheat flour and parched corn and make mush for her family to eat, and for Grandfather and Ze-do, too.

After the store rooms were filled to almost bursting there was more time left for playing and resting. Not all the people had spare time though. Those who had to build houses for Shalako were more than busy. Uncle was one of these. He had to build a new room for he was to entertain one of the Shalako.

Grandfather said that he and Ze-do

were going to be busy at other things for a few days but after that, he told Uncle, "My grandson here, may be free to help you until other work calls." Ze-do wondered what he and Grandfather were going to do next, but Grandfather said he would know in good time.

Grandfather said, "Perhaps tomorrow something will happen."

So Ze-do watched the sunset and the yellow-lost time. He watched the stars come out. He watched the orange-yellow autumn moon rising high from behind the foothills. Then he undid his blanket roll and stretched out on his blankets. Little by little sleep came, coaxing him into the night shadows of not-knowing.

When Ze-do opened his eyes again it was time to go with Grandfather to greet the sun for the new day.

And Grandfather said, "This is the tomorrow that I was telling you about. Come, we have something to do."

He and Ze-do went out of the house and across the plaza and through the narrow passageway between the houses. They went to the cornfield where the horses were eating the cornstalks.

Other Things To Do

Grandfather took Ze-do out to the corn-fields where his and all the other people's horses were eating the dry cornstalks. Other men and big boys were there. They were riding around. They were roping horses. They were having a good time while they were catching the horses that they wanted for the day.

Grandfather roped a horse and mounted. He rode around the pasture looking at all his horses. Then he picked out one of his best ponies. He roped him and told Ze-do to get on and ride.

Ze-do got on, but the horse was wild. No sooner had the boy jumped upon his back than he was off again. Flying through the air he went, and thud, on the hard ground he was sitting. Ze-do felt the top of his head. He thought that his feet must be sticking through. He was surprised to find that they were not. Nothing but the top of his head was there. He picked himself up. All the men were laughing and all the big boys, too.

Grandfather roped the horse again. Ze-do knew what he must do. He did it. Ouch! Again he was sitting on the sharp stubble of the cornfield!

Ze-do tried again and again. At last the horse grew tired. He tossed his head a lit-tle, but that was all. Ze-do rode him all around the pasture.

The men said to Grandfather, "You must have given your Fire Child stick leaf while we were not looking." They said that because if boys are whipped with stick leaf plant they grow strong in holding on to things.

Grandfather laughed with the men. He told them, "Perhaps that is so. Why should it not be true. The stick leaf plant belongs to all the people."

Grandfather said to Ze-do, "If you can break that horse for riding, I will give him to you."

Ze-do was stiff and sore, but he was very happy. On the way home from the corn-fields he told the other boys. "Next week, when my Grandfather gives me my horse, you will see some racing."

Uncle heard him say this. Uncle laughed long and loud. He said, "Next week you won't have broken that horse. It will be a good many weeks before the Old One is ready to give him to you." Ze-do stuck his lips out, as Zuni children do when things do not please them. Grandfather walked in silence, but Uncle sang a little song, and the small boys helped him sing it. After a little more walking Ze-do sang, too. He threw back his head and sang the words loud and clear. Soon his heart was singing.

Then Grandfather smiled at him. He said very low, so that only Ze-do could hear him, "Boys must learn to bear the burden of truth, as a horse learns to bear his saddle. That is the way of things."

"Now I know what you say, my Grandfather. Every day I will ride that horse for as long as it takes."

Grandfather nodded. "Everyday you must ride him until he carries you as his friend."

And Ze-do sang again with Uncle and the small boys.

Night came soon now, and the air of before-dawn was sharp and chill. Days were short. Sun Father seemed over-bright, as if he were trying to push winter backward. The swallows had gone, taking the last of summer. The time of sandstorm winds was upon the people. Their angry wind-hands beat on the house walls and against the blue doors of Zuni. Whirlwinds with witches in their hearts, danced in the sacred plaza, and through the narrow-passageways between the houses.

At last snow came. The snakes were put to sleep. It was story-telling time again.

Summer time in Zuni is not story-telling time. To tell stories in summer is to call the snakes. There are some people who dare to tell stories in summer if they hold a sunflower in their hand all the time they are talking. But Grandfather did not know if sunflowers were special friends to him. He had never been given a sign that they were. So he did not tell stories in summer.

But now that the snow had come and had put the snakes to sleep, Grandfather told stories again. The people came to his house and sat on rolls of blankets before his fireplace. They looked into the dancing fire flames while Grandfather's low voice made word music for them to hear.

Ze-do always sat close beside his Grandfather for everyone knew that these were told for this child who was so close to his heart.

One night Grandfather told the story of the Star People. Grandfather said,
"They say that
    the Supreme One
    the Giver-of-life
    known to A'shi wi
    as He-She
    created the clouds
    and the Great Waters.
They say—Then
    the Rain Priest
    said to the Rain Woman
'I too will create beauty,
    a beautiful something
    to give light at night
    when the Moon Mother sleeps!'
They say
    into the palm of his left hand
    the Rain Priest spat
    and with the fingers of his right hand,
    the Rain Priest patted it.
Like yucca suds the spittle foamed
    forming bubbles of many colors,
    then he blew upwards
    thus creating the stars
    and the constellations."

Grandfather paused; he looked around at the listening people. He looked closely at his Grandchild beside him. Grandfather said, "That is the way it happened, so the ancients have said. I have heard it that way."

Grandfather continued his story.
"The Morning Star
    the Rain Priest called
    the First-Warrior
    who-comes-before-
Sun Father
    At-the-dawn-of-today.

The Dipper
   is known as
   the Seven.
Orion's belt
   is called
   the Row.
The Pleiades
   are beloved.
They are precious.
They are
   the little seed stars.
   They received
   that name
   'long ago when the earth was soft.' "
Grandfather said
   "The Milky Way
   is a holy road."

And he sang them an ancient song of the holy road traveling the heavens.

Grandfather sang songs of Moon Mother, telling how every month she was born anew. He sang songs of the Sun Father's two houses. He called sunrise, "comes-out-standing-to-his-sacred-place," and he called sunset, "goes-in-to-sit-down-at-his-other-sacred-place."

And the nights grew longer in Zuni. Once again, winter had come. Winter, with its snow-hung skies bearing downward. Winter, with its snow-covered mesas pushing inward. Winter, closing around Zuni, shutting the people within their houses.

Knowledge

Snow scattered lightly down from the grandfather snow-clouds, frightened from hiding by the angry shrieking of the terrible god of the North Wind.

The people sat together before the warmth of their fireplaces and the Old Ones opened their hearts.

Ze-do was happy. His mind and body had become one with his days. His thoughts and his acts were fitting the patterns of Zuni living.

Children in other parts of the world may receive praise for thinking differently than those about them, for doing things in a different manner, but this is not true of Zuni children.

Zuni life is patterned, and Zuni children early, learn to live in harmony with that pattern. They learn to think as the ancients have said they must think. They learn to do as it has been done since the beginning.

Ze-do did not, now, fight against things which were so.

He accepted them. He had been taught that long ago, when the earth was soft, the Kachinas came to the village and lived with the people. At this time Zuni customs were formed. When the earth hardened, so did the customs, and both have remained unchanged. From the beginning until the end must they be thus.

These days Grandfather watched Ze-do closely. He saw that the boy was well and strong. He saw that he was brave and uncomplaining. He saw that he was happy, and this last was best, for all Zuni believe that joy is pleasing to the gods, but that sadness offends them.

Now Grandfather spent more and more time alone with the boy, talking to him of things which concerned just them. Ze-do was led more and more to know that his year at home had been a time of training for a special thing. He was led more and more to feel that the great time of his year was coming. He knew that some day he would go back to Government School. He knew that when it came time for choosing life-roads, many would lie before him. But all this was far away. What was important was what was happening now.

Days he had spent alone, in silence and in hunger, had been to strengthen his heart for this which was coming. Days he had spent in doing, in seeing, and in listening, had been to strengthen his mind for this which was coming. Days he had spent in fasting, in running, and training, had been to strengthen his body for this which was coming. Heart and mind and body were now ready.

Grandfather talked long and seriously

67

when only he and his boy were together. He talked of holy things, of gods and their wishes, and gradually, Ze-do understood what was before him.

Near the end of the Zuni year comes their most sacred festival.

Then the gods walk the earth.

Then the gods come among the living.

And Ze-do was told how Zuni men help these in coming.

All night now there was meeting of those men who had been chosen to help the coming of the gods.

Food and sleep were little things to men who walked with gods.

Zuni lay grey and cold and closed within itself in secret mystery.

Forty days passed by.

Then one night the Mud Heads came to Zuni. The Mud Heads are the spirit people, who came back from the spirit world to teach earth people how to play.

The people welcomed their coming by having huge fires in their fireplaces and lighting their out-of-door-ovens to bursting with flames.

The Mud Heads were ten in number. They had funny, round, knobby heads of mud. The knobs were filled with seeds and cotton and dust from the footprints of the people.

They were funny the night they came dancing into the village. They danced in the plazas, and climbed on the housetops, and played pranks, and said things to make the people laugh.

After the Mud Heads had finished their jokes, Grandfather spoke. The people stayed in their houses, because that was the custom, but you could hear them listening.

Grandfather told them, "You are to make yourselves and your houses and all your possessions beautiful, for in eight days you will be visited by my people, the Shalako gods."

Zuni Games

Dancing snowflakes filled the outside air, but within the house all was bright and warm. Piñon and cedar wood burned in the fire-place and the leaping flames were almost sun-bright color.

Grandfather and Ze-do played la-po-chi-wi. Grandfather sat at one side with his back toward the fire and Ze-do sat at the other end of the hearth with his back to the fire. They each had three feathered arrows made of reeds and about as large as pencils. Grandfather threw first. He threw his arrow to the middle of the room. Its sharp point stuck in the dirt floor and it stood there tall and straight, with its feathers waving like a dancer resting. Now it was Ze-do's turn to throw. He was to throw his arrow in such a way that its feathers touched the feathers of Grandfather's arrow. It looked easy to do and if he did it he was to have Grandfather's arrow. The one to get all the arrows would win the game.

Ze-do said, "Oh, Grandfather, will you feel sad if I get all the arrows? We will be just playing, you know. I will give them back to you." Then Ze-do threw his arrow. He threw it so it would touch Grandfather's. It did touch the feathers of Grandfather's arrow, but then it fell down. It did not stand up. It did not look like a dancer

resting. If the throw is good, the arrow will stand up after it touches the enemy arrow. Its sharp point should stick in the dirt floor. Ze-do tried again and again. Grandfather could do it every time, but Ze-do did not do it at all the first night.

Grandfather comforted him. He said that soon he would learn to do it. Grandfather said that when he did learn, they would ask Uncle over to play with them. Then they both laughed because soon Uncle was going to be surprised and lose some arrows.

The little boy and the old man then played the moccasin game. Ze-do placed his moccasins beneath a blanket and hid a bean in one of them. Then Grandfather guessed which little shoe held the bean. Then it was Grandfather's turn to hide the bean and Ze-do's turn to guess. Ze-do was good at guessing. He learned to watch, watch his Grandfather's face and sometimes it would tell him things that his Grandfather did not know it was telling. When Grandfather was guessing, Ze-do closed his face up tight so that it would tell no secrets.

The corncob game of than-ka-la-wi is a good one too. Grandfather and Ze-do could not play it now because it is played only in the spring of the year. But Grandfather explained how it was played. A corn cob is stood on a flat, sandstone rock. A smaller flat rock is put on top of the cob. And on this small top some turquoise beads or some silver buttons are placed. Then the players sit at the far end of the room and throw little round stones at the corncob. If a stone hits on top of the buttons or the beads they belong to the one who threw the stone. Ze-do wished it was spring because he wanted some silver buttons, but he did not say so. It was not the right time to play that game. Nothing could be done about those silver buttons.

Quatsia was very busy helping Uncle build the new room for Shalako. But even though she was busy she took time to do something nice for Ze-do. She made him two red clay balls as large as chicken's eggs. Grandfather showed him how to juggle them. He called juggling it-zu-lu-lu-na-wai. Every Zuni boy learns it-zu-lu-lu-na-wai. They learn how to make cat's cradle, too. Even the girls can make cat's cradles. Long, long ago the Spider Woman, who was grandfather to the twin holy warriors, taught them to make their shields of cat's cradles. Zuni do not call them cat's cradles. They say pich-o-wai-nai.

Snow went away and Sun Father shone again almost as bright as if it were summer. Uncle said that White people called this time of year Indian Summer. He did not know why unless it was that this time of warmth and brightness was a special gift of the sun to the Indians. He said that he thought Indians loved the sun more than White people did.

Uncle said if Grandfather and Ze-do were through with doing other things, now, he could use a little help. Grandfather thought about it and then answered, "Well, for a few days."

So Ze-do began to help Uncle. Other men were helping him, too. They were making a new room. They were making it big and very high. They were making it for Shalako. Shalako is tall. Sometimes, as Ze-do brought a can of paint over to Uncle who was painting a new door, he stopped in the bright sunshine to think of Shalako. Sometimes, as he helped Quatsia plaster with brown earth the sides of the new room, he would look to the far distances where the Shalako were waiting for Shalako time.

Everybody in Zuni, now, was working early and late. There were six new Shalako houses being built for the six Shalako who were coming. At night when it was too dark for working there were strange cries heard in the passageways around the pueblo. There were the low sounds of drums in the underground rooms, and over and over could be heard the voices of singing men.

More and more men came to give their help in building the new room for the Shalako. Faster and faster they worked. More and more came a new feeling into Zuni. A feeling of excitement. A feeling of wonder. A feeling of holiness for Shalako time was drawing near.

Waiting for Shalako

Shalako are the home-blessing gods. They bless the new houses of the people. They are giant bird creatures who come running with their great beaks snapping. They are beautiful. They are sacred. Their coming is the fruit of the Zuni year.

In the new houses where the Shalako are to be entertained there must be a great feast prepared. There must be food enough for the thousand Zuni and the hundreds of visitors who come to view the sacred home-blessing gods.

Uncle killed twenty sheep and five cows and Quatsia had women to help her cut up the meat and cook it. Uncle went to the Trader at the Trading Post. There he bought wagon loads of food and new clothes for himself and Quatsia and her children. All this cost him more than a hundred dollars and he would have to work at the White man's store all next year before he would have money enough to pay it. Shalako time costs the Zuni people money.

All the women in the pueblo plastered the outside of their houses and whitewashed the inside walls. They made new mud floors and washed the windows and painted the doors new blue. If they could, they went to the White man's town and bought chairs and sometimes a table or a bed.

For a week, all day and all night, the women baked bread in the out-of-doors ovens. They cooked beans and chili and boiled meat and parched corn.

In one of the upper terraced houses an old, old blind woman lived. Her house was just one small room with nothing in it but a roll of blankets. In one corner was the fireplace, but it was different from other fireplaces. It was low with a thin, flat, red-hot slab on top. The old woman sat before the fire with a great round bowl of watery blue cornmeal gruel beside her. Hour after hour she would dip her twisted fingers into the bowl and she would spread the dripping watery gruel over the red-hot stone. When it cooked and its edges curled up, deftly she would slip her fingers under and slip it from the stone. She would curl it into a thin roll. This is called paper bread and it is as thin as paper. Sometimes a laughing girl would climb the ladders to the old woman's house with a new bowl of gruel upon her head. And sometimes a young man came with more wood for the fireplace to keep the stone red hot. The blind old woman never burned her fingers. She never burned the bread. But all day long, hour after hour, her fingers moved like a song with three notes. They dipped into the gruel. They dripped over the red-hot stone. They rolled up the thin sheets of paper bread. And she was old. And she was blind.

Everyone works before Shalako time.

At last all the new houses were finished and all the old houses were cleaned and freshened. At last all the new clothes had been made, shirts and pants, moccasins and dresses, belts and hair ties. At last all the sheep and cows had been killed, all the corn had been ground into meal, all the cooking had been done.

Soon now the Shalako would come. All the Zuni house doors were closed. All the Zuni house windows were darkened. Zuni people were making their hearts ready. Zuni people were thinking holy thoughts. Zuni people were praying.

One day, two days, three days went by. Time paused in Zuni as the people made ready for Shalako.

All was quiet. All was still. All doors were closed. The people sat within their houses, letting their hearts talk.

On the fourth day the visitors began coming. White people came in cars and buses. They came from the ranches and towns nearby. They came from far-off places, from countries across the Great-Waters, from the place of Washington, where lives the Great White Father. Navajo and Hopi came on horseback and in wagons, many hundreds in number. Smaller groups of other kinds of Indians came.

White people walked through the narrow passageways. They looked about them. They smiled and talked, and were friendly and curious. Indians lounged against the walls, they squatted in sunny corners. Sometimes they smoked, sometimes they spoke, but mostly, they were looking and thinking.

Zuni that had been so still was not so still now. Zuni that had been so quiet was not quiet now, or closed within itself or empty.

Zuni was crowded with people, with different kinds of people. Zuni air was thick with talking in different kinds of languages. Zuni babies hid behind their mother's blankets. Zuni dogs crouched against walls and sniffed the new smells with suspicion.

A far-away drum was heard; not so much in sound as in earth vibration.

The air beat with distant song, so far away; it was felt more than heard.

Time dragged.

They were waiting for Shalako.

Shalako

With the morning star of before-the-dawn-of-Shalako-day, black figures moved in groups and singly out through the shadow-filled passageways, across the river and on into the grey-darkened distance. They went to the Shalako House.

They were the men who had been chosen to help in the coming of the gods.

Ze-do was with them, and by his side was his ceremonial father.

With the rising sun, Zuni threw open its doors. More and more visitors came into the pueblo. By noon, expectancy had reached high pitch. All through the short, clear, cold afternoon excitement grew.

Waiting was a part of the drama of the coming of the gods.

White people walked around restlessly, feeding their impatience for the great moment to arrive. Indians were calm. They knew when it was time for the gods to come, they would come. Meanwhile it was good to wait. They accepted waiting as part of the enjoyment of the day.

Sun Father moved through the heavens in slow, serene majesty. The afternoon grew old, and a cold wind blew.

Then a moment of silence which broke into happening.

From the Shalako House
   from the Zuni Great Plain
   came the little Fire God
   the Shula wi'tsi.
Dressed in black,
   with black helmet
   and spotted
   in sun colors,
   red
   yellow
   blue
   and white,
   he came.
Carrying a fawnskin bag
   of the seeds
   of the squash
   and the different colored corns
   and the water gourds,
   he came.
With feathers
   on his head
   and small game
   on his back
   carrying
   a blackened fire-brand,
   and feathered sticks,
   he came,
   the little Fire God,
   the Shula wi'tsi.
Before him walked
   his ceremonial father
   with white blanket
   of deerhide

with white leggings
of deerhide
with white moccasins
of deerhide.
Carrying
a basket of prayer plumes,
before the little Fire God
walked the ceremonial father.
Across the bridge of the river
came
the little Fire God.
Before him walked
his ceremonial father.
The people gathered
on the banks of the river
to watch them coming.
The people parted
to make a road
to let them through.
The people blessed them
as they passed
with sacred cornmeal.
To the Shalako houses
they went.
To the house of the Mud Heads
they went.
To the house
of the Rain God of the North
they went,
and planted prayer plumes
in their passing.
Then the little Fire God
and his ceremonial father
went back
to the Shrine
of the Middle-of-the-World
to lead
the Council of the Gods
across the bridge of the river;
to lead
the Council of the Gods
into Zuni.

The people watched them. The people followed them. They lined up against the walls of the dancing rooms. They sat in the connecting room looking in through the windows. They crowded close together, but they were quiet. They had deep reverence. These were gods.

Everyone went from house to house, Zuni and visiting Indians and Whites. They stood side by side, sat side by side, walked side by side, watching the coming of the holy ones.

The setting sun rays
painted Sacred Mountain
with fire,
painted the snow patches
with fire,
painted the earth houses
with fire.
To the Shrine
of the Middle-of-the-world,
planted with prayer sticks,
marked with cornmeal,
came the Shalako,
giant bird creatures
with huge beaks snapping,
with huge eyes rolling,
with tiny feet running;
came the Shalako
to the Shrine
of the Middle-of-the-world.

Then the crowds of watching people went there and stood before the Shrine while the giant god-creatures did their running, bird-like dance. After the ceremonies at the Shrine, the six great gods crossed the river into Zuni.

Each with two men attending
out of the fire mists
of sunset,
out of the dusk mists
of evening,

from the Shrine
of the Middle-of-the-world
came the Shalako
crossing the bridge of the river.

Once again the people parted to let them through. Once again the people stood silent and reverent, blessing with cornmeal the messengers of the gods walking among them. Each of the six Shalako went to the house which had been prepared for him, and each was followed by a part of the crowd of visitors.

The Council of the Gods and the little Fire God and his ceremonial father went to the house prepared for them. They were met at the door by Uncle and Quatsia, his wife, by Grandfather, the Sun Priest, and the Rain Priests.

On the floor at one end of the new room which Uncle had built there now was an altar of painted cornmeal and sacred objects. Uncle welcomed the holy visitors. Quatsia, and Grandfather, and the Rain Priests welcomed them. The Holy Ones replied, blessing the children of the house.

Grandfather and another Priest stood before the altar holding flat baskets. Into these baskets the little Fire God emptied his fawnskin bag of the seeds of the squash, the different colored corns, and the water gourds. Across the top of the baskets he put the small game which he had brought with him. These baskets were laid at the foot of the altar.

Then the flute-player,
    the maker
    of sacred wind music,
    sent forth
    his flute song
    from behind
    the altar.
Then the drummer,

    the maker
    of sacred music
    of thunder,
    sent forth his drum song
    from before the altar.
And the patter
    of rain song,
    of rattles
    and whirling of rhombres,
    tied together
    with the men's voices
    of the choir,
    sent forth their songs
    from near the altar.
And the gods ran about
    marking with sacred meal
    the walls of the room,
    the floors of the room,
    the heart of the room,
    its altar.

The room became unbearably crowded, and close, and thick, with the many smells, but the people stayed there watching the gods.

After the gods had finished their marking, Sun Priest seated them in their order on the blanket-covered ledges about the room. Fire God and his ceremonial father sat nearest the altar. Sun Priest sat facing the little Fire God.

Then the seed baskets were taken from the altar and passed down the line of gods and priests, each one breathing his prayers upon them. The small game was blessed, and the women of the house cooked it for the dawn feast.

For the next two hours the gods chanted the litany of the home-blessing prayer. The gods chanted it and the priests responded.

Then the women came in with baskets and bowls of food on their heads. They served the gods the best that the earth-

77

people of Zuni had to offer them. They served them meat stew and peaches and sliced watermelon.

The Fire God took pieces of wafer bread and on them placed other foods, and buried these outside with the prayer plumes under the house ladder.

Then the gods blessed the food and ate it. They blessed all Zuni by eating its food.

After the food was eaten the gods danced. Up and down the crowded room they danced to chanting, to music, to songs, and breathlessly, all Zuni watched them.

What the Council of the Gods did at the house that was prepared for them was being done in all the other houses. The Shalako were at each of their six houses. The Mud Heads were at their houses.

Dancing teams of the different fraternities of the pueblo went about from house to house. They gave dances which they had learned, for the entertainment of the people.

All night there was dancing at Zuni. The Council of the Gods danced. The Mud Heads danced. The Shalako danced. The members of the dancing teams danced.

At sunrise the dawn prayers were said at every house. The people went out of the houses. They went out into the cold, new morning. They went that the dancers might rest.

The doors were closed.

In mid-morning the Fire God led the Council of the Gods across the bridge at the river to the sandy stretch on the other side.

The Shalako came from their houses and crossed the river bridge.

The Mud Heads stayed closed within Zuni.

On the sandy stretch of the river the Council of the Gods planted prayer plumes, and departed across the Zuni great plain, out of sight among the foothills.

The Shalako planted their prayer plumes, and they raced in the sand. Then they too, left Zuni and went the way of the gods.

Shalako was finished.

The gods were gone.

And only those who had received initiation knew what moving force had borne the gods to earth again.

Long ago, both the gods and the dead came often to Zuni, but that was when men's hearts were pure.

Now, the dead come as Mud Heads, in the spirit of fun, and the gods and their messengers come in mystery.

Zuni went back to everyday living, thinking not that the gods were gone. But rather that the gods came. They walked among the earth people letting them live again, for a night, with sacred Shalako.

Back To The Middle-Place

Indian Summer was long gone and winter snows fell steadily. The Zuni world was blanketed in whiteness and in stillness. Each dawn Grandfather went again to the petrified tree stump to note the shadows of the sun. Ze-do went with him. He did not mind the snow and the dark and the cold. It was all part of the trail of living, like rocks were part of the trail of Sacred Mountain.

Grandfather was often silent and sometimes he looked sad. Ze-do tried hard to please him, he tried to bring back the smile to the kind old eyes. He stayed close to him all day and slept near him at night. This wise old man was dear to him.

One day Grandfather went into his inner room and stayed in there for a long time. When he came out he brought three Navajo rugs with him. He went to Uncle's house and talked with Uncle and with Quatsia. When he came back Uncle was with him. Uncle brought a bridle and a pottery jar that Quatsia had made. He put them with the Navajo rugs. He looked teasingly at Ze-do. "I am going to town for the Grandfather," he said.

"You? I am the one to do things for the Grandfather," Ze-do told him. Uncle looked more teasing than ever. "Not this time."

"I could go to help you with the horses." But Uncle answered, "Not this time."

Ze-do looked at Grandfather. He hoped Grandfather would see his mistake, but Grandfather did not do anything. He stood waiting in the doorway while Uncle went for his horses and his wagon. When Uncle came with them Grandfather put the rugs and the bridle and the pottery in the wagon underneath the seat. He said, "It must be a good one." Uncle nodded. He looked at Ze-do. "You are to get wood for Quatsia while I am gone."

The horses and the wagon and Uncle went around the pueblo to the road that leads to town. Soon they were out of sight. Grandfather went back into his inner room and after awhile Ze-do went to Quatsia's house to see how badly wood was needed.

The day went by and the next and the next one. Snow melted and thawed. The ground was springy with dampness. Quasia used too much wood. Ze-do said to himself that if she would stay out of doors she could keep warm without a fire. It would have done no good to say such things to Quatsia. But he did say to his Grandfather, "That man is too good to his wife." But Grandfather did not agree with him. He said that was the way it should be. Ze-

do was surprised. He thought that being men together, they could understand such things.

For three days he had done nothing but carry wood. Well, almost nothing but carry wood.

On the third day it began to snow again. When Ze-do had finished bringing wood for Quatsia he brought some for Grandfather. He went back for more and more until a high pile of pinon and cedar boughs and twigs were beside Grandfather's door. He felt proud of his work and big and strong. It was good to feel that one was taking care of others.

After it was dark, as he and Grandfather were sitting beside the fire eating tortillas and drinking hot, strong coffee, the dogs began to bark. Soon they heard the creaking of Uncle's wagon outside. Uncle came in to warm himself at Grandfather's fire. Ze-do went out to unhitch the horses, to feed them and put them in the night corral.

When he came back Uncle was gone and Grandfather was looking into the flames of his fireplace. Ze-do put his wet moccasins to dry. He warmed his brown feet. He unrolled his blankets and went to sleep.

Before dawn he awakened to go with his Grandfather.

Outside there were no stars. Black night hung low. The white snow piled thick on the sand and the pinon shrubs and the lonesome fields.

Two figures walked in the trail. One was tall, the other one was short. Both were wrapped in black blankets. Only their eyes peeped out. Only their moccasins seemed to move. They walked quickly. They were part of the night.

When they reached the edge of the Zuni village they waited for the sun. They did not talk. They did not break the stillness of the world.

The clouds of night parted to show the colors of new day. The sun came through. The old man and the little boy gave the sunrise prayer together. It sounded like one voice, but it was made up of two people speaking.

Stillness was broken. The things of the world began to move and to make noise. Day had begun.

Grandfather turned to Ze-do, "It is almost Winter Solstice," he said, "the sun is almost at the Middle-Place again."

Grandfather held something in his hand. He held it out to Ze-do. "I sent Uncle to the town for this. It is for you."

Ze-do took the little package. It was a little white box. He opened it. There was cotton, like snow wrapping. He looked beneath. There was a watch, a watch the color of the sun.

Grandfather said, "T'anta, sun measure. To measure your days as the White man does, but to remind you forever of Sun Father who gives you the sun."

Ze-do held the beautiful sun-yellow t'anta in his hand. He could not speak. His heart was too full.

Gradfather went on talking. "Our Zuni year is over, Fire Child. They gave you to me to teach you the ways of your people. I have taught you much that I know."

Ze-do was frightened. "But Grandfather. . .Grandfather. . ."

The old man would not listen. He took the boy by the hand. "Little son of my heart, you must go. I promised to send you back at the end of the year. I promised to send you back to the school of the White man."

"Oh Grandfather, my Grandfather. . ."

Grandfather pointed outward. "In the

83

days of tomorrow your trail will fork again. It may lead out into the unknown. It may turn backward to Zuni. I do not know. I know only that now it is time to go. Do not wait until they come for you. Go now. Do not look back."

Sun Father rode the heavens. Sky and earth were red with his coming. The snow looked like blood.

Ze-do walked alone into the brightness of new day. He looked little, wrapped in his black blanket, walking slowly over the trail that led to school.

The sun-yellow t'anta in his hand went tick, tick, tick measuring the hours of day. And his heart beneath his blanket went beat, beat, beat, measuring the span of life.

Grandfather removed his head band, for that is necessary in time of deep prayer. He looked after the black-clad figure, trudging along so bravely in the snow. Grandfather prayed. At the end he spoke:

"I have sent forth my prayers.
I have given to my Grandchild
The showing-how.
He has learned
to bend his thoughts.
Now he goes forth
into the wilderness.
May his road lie in safety.
May his road lie in goodness,
and strength,
And beauty.
May his road be fulfilled.
I have sent forth my prayers."

Ze-do was but a little black speck in the distance. Grandfather turned toward Zuni. There were things to do. One thought comforted his hurting heart. Sun Father traveled the world. Sun Father would enfold the Fire Child of the Sun Priest.

The Artist Speaks For Himself

I was born at Zuni Pueblo where I enjoyed my childhood life with my parents and two brothers.

I started school at Zuni Day School and stayed there three years. Then I went to school at Black Rock, about four miles from the Zuni village. The third year I was there, the school was discontinued. At that time I went back to the Zuni Day School again.

There, as a student with my classmates, I was told to do some painting. That was the very first time I ever tried painting. When the teacher saw my work she thought I was just naturally good in painting from the very beginning.

The next thing I remember all the teachers admired my work, for at that time I painted some murals at the school building and at the hospital at Black Rock. They are still there.

Leaving the Zuni Day School, I went to other schools. I was glad to see the different schools and wanted to know which school was best to be in. At eighteen years of age I went to Albuquerque Indian School where I studied art under an art teacher. I improved a lot there.

I completed high scool in 1940 and after graduating I returned home, thinking that I woudl help my folks with the farm work.

During the summer I was invited to go to Santa Fe Indian School in the fall to do some more work in art. That was the time I illustrated this book by Mrs. Clark, which of course I enjoyed doing.

Soon after graduating from art school at Santa Fe I married a Taos girl and now am making my home with my family at Taos, which is called the "Art Center of the Southwest."

At present I paint with water colors, oil, charcoal, and chalk. Besides painting pictures to sell, I have a farm of my own. I have won several first and second prizes for my paintings during the Gallup ceremonials and at state fairs in Albuquerque, New Mexico.

Percy Tsisete Sandy
Taos, New Mexico